The Deconstruction of Wesley Smithson

ALSO BY SARAH MURPHY

The Measure of Miranda
Comic Book Heroine

THE DECONSTRUCTION OF WESLEY SMITHSON

A COLLECTION OF FICTION

Sarah Murphy

The Mercury Press

§

ACKNOWLEDGEMENTS

I would like to acknowledge the financial support of both the Canada Council and the Alberta Foundation for the Literary Arts in the writing of this collection. Thanks also to Leila Sujir for her belief in the voice of Wesley Smithson, and for the work we did together on the performance/panel at the Blurring Genres Conference at the University of Calgary, for which the piece, "Paramilitary Parafictions," was developed. It should be noted that this piece first appeared in published form in *(f.)Lip*, Vol. 3, No. 2, and also appeared in *TESSERA*, Winter, 1991, along with a description of the panel performance.

And, as always, many thanks to all the others who have supported me in my work, to Beverley Daurio my editor, and in particular, to my partner, Tom Proudlock.

The publisher gratefully acknowledges the financial assistance of the Canada Council and the Ontario Arts Council, as well as that of the Ontario Ministry of Culture and Communications through the Ontario Publishing Centre.

Cover design: Ted Glaszewski
Cover photograph: Paul Till
Production co-ordination: The Blue Pencil
Composition in Berkeley and Gill Sans by TASK.
Printed and bound in Canada.

Canadian Cataloguing in Publication:

Murphy, Sarah
The deconstruction of Wesley Smithson
ISBN 0-920544-94-0
I. Title.
PS8576.U764D42 1992 C813'.54 C92-094537-6
PR9199.3.M876D42 1992

Canadian Sales Representation: The Literary Press Group.
Distributed in Canada by General Publishing.

The Mercury Press
137 Birmingham Street, Stratford, Ontario
Canada N5A 2T1

Contents

Cassie, Cassie 9

Paramilitary Parafictions 55

The Deconstruction of Wesley Smithson 71

Dedication

The year of the publication of this collection, 1992, marks five hundred years from the events that started the devastation of the lives and cultures of the First Nations of the Americas. For that reason I would like to ask the reader to take a moment before beginning the reading of this book, to remember and to mourn the myriad voices that have been and will be silenced in that ongoing holocaust, the myriad stories left forever without tellers.

And to celebrate those voices left moving among us, I would like to dedicate this small collection of untellings to my Dad, who raised me after my father's untimely death, William (Bill) Doyle Sherar, of the Choctaw Nation, a people dispossessed of their lands and forced to walk the Trail of Tears in the United States circa 1836.

Bill, a seaman by trade, now retired, spent much of his time on his voyages around the world following the routes pioneered by Columbus and by Magellan, collecting those stories and histories that he could find of aboriginal dispossession, survival, and occasional, if too often short-lived, triumph. For the part he has played, invisible like that of so many generations of oral storytellers, in keeping those stories alive to inform the future, I would like to thank him.

And to thank him too, for his part in giving me a voice, and making me a storyteller.

Cassie, Cassie

ANOTHER MESSAGE IS ABOUT TO START, there is less and less doubt in Polly's mind. She has learned to read the signs though she is not at all sure that Mother, who will receive the message, can say the same.

Such messages were supposed to become less frequent up here in the middle of the mountains, Polly is sure of that, everyone said Mother would feel better with the fresh air and the relative peace, the absolute security, the few people about, except weekends, and most of them laughing. Large open faces, tanned or burned, wide-eyed would be the best way to describe them, the few times you actually looked them in the face, mostly on the lift lines, yes, wide-eyed and cheerful, two good adjectives, Polly is sure she will use them in her journal, or maybe on a postcard to a friend back in school. Having a wonderful time here in Canada, at the resort, all the people here are wide-eyed and cheerful, a good turn of phrase though she wonders a minute if it also applies to the Japanese tourists, she thinks they are Japanese, the question is whether orientals are ever wide-eyed, which doesn't matter too much, if she just says: What a marvellous change. It will sound very good, certainly wise beyond her years, and the truth is that she's enjoying it, very much in fact, to be so far up on top of the world, she can feel it even now as Mother sits down and props her skis up, a cross in the snow though she has not fallen, she's just sitting there waiting right in front of a tree, they have made it down to the edge of the tree line, where for a moment there is silence.

God Polly this cramp again, and then silence. One moment of silence while the howling of the groups of people stops long enough to make an opening in the world, a declaration perhaps, Polly is not sure, from the earth itself to let people know where they are, the precise weight of the ball of atmosphere above them, its contrast to the weight, the density, of upthrust rock here on the Continental Divide. It seems so clear that Polly can feel it, this exact place that contains all the geography lessons that tell how water condenses out and begins to flow, here from this point into two watersheds, so that she sees glaciers and droplets and streams and lakes and rivers and more lakes and finally the ocean, with the snow dunes around her suddenly breakers and the sun as bright as the fire in Mother's face. While Polly slowly finds herself coming to believe, after all it's what Cassie has told her, that the earth is claiming responsibility for this act, as its brief and total silence makes the room needed for the message's delivery.

Which will not change Polly's mind about the vacation, she is quite sure about that, her parents were right when they decided it was time to get away, for a little while anyway, making that decision to take her out of boarding school for six months to be with Mother, there was absolutely nothing wrong with that, any more than there had been with putting her in the boarding school in the first place, when things started getting difficult at home, with Cassie acting the way she did. And running away like that after telling Polly so much, things her parents definitely didn't want her to hear, it was Cassie who had always recited at the dinner table,

> **["The Walrus and the Carpenter**
> **Walked on a mile or so,"]**

statistics and stories and finally that poem, that's how Polly had learned it, though maybe she already knew it from childhood, it was just that Cassie always repeated it when Father or Mother started to speak, to explain to Cassie why she was just plain wrong-headed with those things she was doing, telling her why she really did need help, how she must stop trying to make Polly believe she was right; they knew Cassie was doing that, with all those whisperings. While they told Cassie again and again as if they were petting her, petting them both, that everything was really all right, so different from what she thought, then added, their voices only slightly harder, suddenly more steel than aluminum, that it didn't matter what she chose to believe or do, that was up to her. But she still had to understand that Polly was just plain too young to be hearing about those things, she was still a child. Which is what made it very easy for Polly to understand why one day Mother should take her out to lunch, a very marvellous French restaurant, where all the waiters called Mother "Madame" and kind of bowed when they said it and Polly became "Mademoiselle" and wore gloves even though she played surreptitiously with her tableware while Mother pulled out all those pamphlets, and pointed out each special feature, as Polly pretended to look at them, while trying to make out the features of the city roofs obscured by the smog, so many storeys below.

Just as now she tries to make out the shapes farther down the mountain, with the moment of silence over as Mother moans and Polly hears a shout far away as people race each other, older boys she is sure from the tone of the whoop, the kind Mother just calls: Too old for you, Polly. All of them in blues and reds, it is the women who wear the unusual colours, the purples and the pinks and the greens, even yellow sometimes, them and the telemarkers,

> **["And then they rested on a rock,**
> **Conveniently low:"]**

there don't seem to be any of those this year, and they always stand out, kneeling as if in prayer in their modified brown hiking boots. The kind she'd seen on people just like them, in that country they had once gone to, she and her family, the one way up in other greener mountains with natives as unmoving as the trees, while the hikers laughed and twittered like birds alighting among them here and there to leave perfect boot prints in the imperfect mud, as their heads darted about to take it all in, to buy things and laugh again: Oh the fresh air, the view, the colours, they said, their voices carrying in the rarefied atmosphere,

> **["And all the little Oysters stood**
> **And waited in a row."]**

so much higher than here but not as cold, all the snow was on the slopes above. Except one place like this where the family skied in the same air that went on forever so that Polly could imagine she was breathing it, the same air, exactly that same air the messages would come through, though she doesn't know if that's where they originate, or in some other place, Cassie hadn't been clear about that even if she'd run away there too.

While Mother takes off her boot, her face contorted from the pain, and words continue playing in Polly's mind,

> **["'The time has come,' the Walrus said,**
> **'To talk of many things:"]**

as she tries to figure out why this message now, and why the poem goes with it, because there was no message that first time when she let it play in her mind, just let it go on and on, no message she could notice anyway, it was just sadness she saw on Mother's face, there was no pain, and the poem actually helped that day of her decision, to pick that school, there was no more reason to have gone there than the fact that the particular pamphlet was in her mother's hand at the moment the voice in her mind reached the part about the Walrus' talk, and her fork went to her mouth in anticipation of the end, of the poem and the meal, because they hadn't yet, she and Mother, they hadn't eaten anything at all, not even ordered their food and the talk Mother was giving only took into consideration all the advantages she would have,

> **["Of shoes— and ships— and sealing-wax—**
> **Of cabbages— and kings"]**

it had nothing to do with sealing wax much less cabbages or kings. Although maybe with kings' daughters, or princes, maybe it was princes' daughters Mother said went there, and some of them looked like cabbages, maybe that was the connection that started the poem because it definitely made her giggle so that Mother had looked at her, the eyes registering horror, the unspoken words that said: Oh, no, it can't be happening to her, not her too, as Mother smiled indulgently and patted Polly's hand telling herself that: Yes, it must be the excitement of going to the same school with princes' daughters and the daughters of important statesmen, of generals too, new and different but the right class for Father's second and perhaps only daughter, it is so hard to know now, but a school with good food and better teachers, such a rich environment, so much to take in: It will be such a good experience for you, Polly, you'll meet girls like you from all over the world, emphasizing the, *Like you*, making sure Polly knew they were all like her, with Father an adman: That's more important than you know these days, Father always said, rubbing his hands together: We're right in the centre of it all, it was time his daughter took her place among all those other daughters whose fathers came to him to make everything all right, and there would be other things too: Singing and dancing, the ballet, Mother said, languages and special skills: What every young lady should know, she went on and pressed Polly's hand,

> **["And why the sea is boiling hot—**
> **And whether pigs have wings.'"]**

squeezing harder and harder as her face became sad and drawn and her eyes looked away while other words came out: What we should have done for Cassie, to give her other interests. Polly remembers Mother saying those words and the tears in the corners of Mother's eyes, and how she changed the subject right away afterward, talking faster and faster about how Polly would learn architecture if she ever wanted to design her own house the way Mother had, carpentry if she wanted to build it, interior decorating if she wanted to arrange it, upholstery if she wanted to make the furniture, horticulture for the greenhouse, floriculture for the livingroom, ornithology to raise songbirds, entomology to raise crickets, etymology to impress the guests admiring the view from the livingroom. Anything she could think of that might stop Polly from noticing she was being sent away so that she didn't catch whatever it was they thought Cassie had.

Because they hadn't dared send Cassie away the way she was, she wouldn't go with princes or princes' daughters, she just wouldn't match, Mother was convinced Cassie wouldn't go with the design or the decoration or the paintings or the furniture, or even the songbirds though her voice was like theirs, repeating and repeating the same pattern the same few notes in her mad ramblings certainly she didn't go with the dinner parties Mother planned so carefully, there was no longer any place for her to sit: But where will I put her, Mother kept saying: She can't go between General and Mrs. between President and Mrs. between Doctor and Mrs. between Engineer and Mrs. between Reverend and Mrs., Mother had taken to repeating before they locked Cassie in the maid's room because they couldn't send her away somewhere else either: She's our daughter, Polly heard Mother say to Father when she thought Polly wasn't listening: We should protect her. Until the day Father said: She's no daughter of mine.

And then it no longer mattered that Cassie couldn't or wouldn't protect herself. Because she might have something to do with those messages with those threats with what had happened to Mother. Reciting over and over and making Polly repeat after her even if Polly had always hated that little ditty about the Oysters: It's better if you do, Cassie had said: It's like taking your medicine, the more you hate it the better it works, laughing as Polly remembered how awful she'd felt as a young child when Mother still read out loud to her, it had made her shiver until she had nightmares. Of those two walking arm in arm along the beach talking and telling all those stories to their little friends, the ones they called their friends in their oily voices, oil enough to swallow them down anyway with only the oldest wise enough not to go, or perhaps too tired, just of all the hullabaloo, Polly never knew, how the youngsters, all those little fatsoes hurried up too dumb to know what was going on so many of them trooping along as the two winked at each other, she can still see them doing it, wink wink as the poem refuses to leave her, even if she's pushed it away, silenced it from her mind, refused that disembodied drowning voice, the way she always tries to no matter what Cassie said. Still, she can't get rid of them, they're always there, those two, smiling at the edge of her vision, ready to stuff themselves, both of them, and after promising to explain how the world worked, that was what they had promised wasn't it? or at least one had, that was what it meant didn't it, that talk of many things: that's what that colon meant didn't it? complete explanation to follow, even if in the poem it was just whether or not pigs had wings or was it fish, back then Polly could never remember, only how sick she felt after, bloated the way she did after lobster or a day at the beach, with a constant red hum that would last the night, and into the day, to be brought on again by words and by shellfish and by tongues licking ice-cream as she refused the words that had told them, that would tell her, cute little things, in her dreams she was always a cute little thing with an oyster-shell bonnet and bright new patent leather shoes, that when you finally understood the explanation you would no longer be there to be satisfied with it. Because you would already be swallowed. Which was the explanation. At least that's what Cassie called it later: The Full and Complete Explanation of How the World Works, as she made Polly recite just once more: All you'll ever really need to know. Just ask Father. You follow me because I promise you a beautiful explanation then I eat you while you smile and ask for the explanation then I burp which is beautiful for me and is your explanation. Only you're not there to listen.

And Cassie would laugh. In those days she laughed a lot. While Polly tended to cry, or throw up.

Listening to that poem and the way Cassie would recite it, over and over in their room with a nasty grin that Polly thought was just to get her, just to make her sick: Oh, you're too soft Polly, Cassie would say: Just like an oyster without a shell, I'd be the oldest oyster myself, if you left it up to me, going on like that, a morbid joke long before the poem became a singsong or a catechism recited like Grace before dinner or over and over in public; or like a lesson as she made Polly learn it, so that back then the poem had already made it terribly hard for Polly to listen at the table. Among all those empty plates and dishes and ones half full as the mouths opened and closed the throats swallowed, male adams' apples going up then down, up then down, greasy female lips being patted gently with colour coordinated napkins as jewelry jingled while Polly tried so hard not to hear Father's explanations of the newest ad campaigns, though she didn't dare plug her ears, just rub them a little, which didn't help because she heard the words anyway, even if she asked Mother a question the explanations would still be made, to the house guests, or even the wine glasses, as the guests or even Mother would chime in too, though never quite so vulgar as the Carpenter with his appeals for slices of bread without so much as a please, just talk about why good advertising was so necessary these days, people just had to understand, with the return explanations spoken exactly the same way, to the centre of the table as if each one had selected a dish to persuade, using very clean terms of course, medical mostly, there was so much to explain, about cancers excised, tumours irradiated, germs flushed out of systems, the difficulty of immunization against some problems, though they always added too that it was a dirty business, all the Doctors seemed to feel that way, though Polly could never figure out which was a Doctor of what, Law or Medicine or Engineering or Propaganda or Political Science or Sociology or Environmental Design or Communications or Biology or Chemistry, all of them talking of the blood and pus of problems that became clean as soon as they were taken care of.

As they spoke of the conduct of the War while Polly's eyes went from adams' apples to mouths, never watching the ones who were talking, but the ones who were swallowing, not what came out but what went in. With her nausea rising as she noted how comfortable they were, how they seemed to wiggle down into their chairs and wave their fat ringed fingers, they couldn't all be fat, she knew that, but it was what she remembered, fingers waving about like the tentacles of sea anemones, the ones Mother kept in the sea aquarium against the wall, or sea weed, the antennae of the shrimp that peeked around the coral, until she shivered, and felt like she was breathing the Perrier water in front of her, or her own blood, as she looked around for Cassie because she didn't understand the explanation, not any of the explanations, and she wanted the one person who'd ever really tried to talk to her. Only by the time she looked Cassie wasn't there. And didn't know the explanation, Polly told herself that, Cassie just made things up. Anyway.

Because Cassie only knew the results. Which was why when Cassie came back that time they started to be afraid to have house guests. You just never knew what she might say. Polly can still hear Mother's voice saying that: You just never know what Cassie might say, bursting out with that childish poem like that right in the middle of something important, as Mother giggled and carefully placed the little bowls with the passion flowers that opened and closed in one day, she knew where to put them even if she didn't know where to put Cassie: They're so marvellous, she said, lasting only one day in their cut crystal bowls, never wilting but just sealing themselves off from the world, from the water and the air, even the movement stately and stiff and slow as all those lovely parts that made the flower so distinctive held themselves together inside rubbing one against the other, the sepals and petals, the filaments and the overshadowing ovary, held up as if on a pedestal in the centre of the tall column that ended in golden anthers and freckled stigmas like three overshadowing arms, that made Mother say: I think of Father each time I look at them, how he shelters us, until one day Cassie giggled and Mother turned bright red. While later when the two girls were in the greenhouse Cassie laughed again and said, conspiratorial: See Polly, they're mini-penises, lemon green mini-dinks, Mother turns red at the sight of even the littlest prick, as she held one out to Polly to examine closely while Polly only looked on in surprise, what could her sister mean, with her little dance step as she laughed about green coloured mini-dicks with wine coloured freckles: Maybe they're Martian, she said, Martian mini-cocks, and she told the joke about the Martian shaking hands that ended this is the way we make love only she held out the bloom for Polly to shake and said: It would be so right if their hands looked like that, and laughed again, still finding only surprise on her sister's face. Because all the dinks Polly had ever seen, on the sons of the General or Engineer or any of Doctors, when they'd played Paramedics or Interrogators, tying each other up, were small and impossibly worm-like, so that her mouth remained slack and open, her personal computer, that's what they called their minds, my zillion megabyte PC they bragged at school, wouldn't even issue the command to shut it until she received further information, waiting until Cassie finally turned red too: Oh, I forgot, she said her hand over her mouth now: Of course, you've never seen them like that, a dink at the ready, and she'd shaken Polly trying to move her from her incomprehension: Run program Polly, come on, she said: Ready to do it, silly, you know about that, don't you? doing it, they have heads like that when they're ready to do it, repeating: Run program Polly, until she'd finally had to do it herself, put another program in Polly's computer, that's how she always called it when she explained things to her little sister: I'm gonna insert a new program, Polly, at least until she'd stopped believing in computers and believed only in that poem, so that this time she said: Here comes the doing it program Polly, and she'd explained the whole thing, using the flowers as visual aids for the details of erect penises and doing it, adding little details as to where and when she'd done it, though not with whom, the way the girls at Polly's school spend all their time talking about doing it, how and where and when and who has and who hasn't, so that Polly was happy she'd found out, that she'd known when they'd started to talk, that she didn't have to ask the way one girl had, who'd been teased for days, she really thought Mother should have told her, instead of just turning red, though maybe that was because Father had been mentioned, she didn't want Polly to connect the details of the program to her and Father, she wanted the bloom to signify something else, not sexual but sweet like its perfume, the way she will still say it is absolutely magnificent the way the blooms close up and seal the members in, anthers and filaments and petals and stigmas, sealed in by the sepals inside the corolla, combining the botany lesson with an analogy to the best families inside their houses while Mother held the closed bloom in her hand with more affection than she showed for the magnificence of the open flower: Sheltered until they fruit, how magnificent, while Polly thought in horror, sheltered until they're ready to be eaten, and strengthened her resolve to eat less, even if they both knew that cut or uncut the flowers almost never came to fruit in the greenhouse, though Mother still looked on the hermetic bloom with impossible tenderness just as Polly still recoiled: I like to imagine their life inside their house, Mother said.

While when the bloom was open Mother would only joke that the guests would be able to see if they had overstayed their welcome: When the bloom has closed they've definitely been here too long, Polly, with Polly staring and staring at the blooms trying to see them start to close, the stigmas move upward to signal the end to the evening, the moment when she could feel sheltered in the corolla of her bed and wouldn't have to listen any more. Not to the explanations, or to Cassie reciting. Though all she ever saw was the small ripples in the water of the glasses as someone lifted a fork, a ripple that became a vision of all those uniformed young men and women, grey or green or brown or black leather like mussels marching off to be eaten, who sang the songs on Father's posters, We serve you best, We fight harder, Our gift is the future while the forks gleamed and received their gifts upon their tines, as the voices went on and on explaining, they couldn't seem to stop, they mustn't want to see it in their minds, feel the pain, Polly would think, the way the Oysters must have shaken themselves as the lemon was squeezed on, shaken themselves and known, right at that moment known. What it was. The pain and the pain to come. The way Mother does now, her pain and her pain to come as she massages her foot, knowing that this message will soon be absolutely unbearable. Her face grey and sculptured, its different planes suddenly hard like the planes of the mountains. The colours the same too.

Not the passion flower purple and green and wine of the suit Mother had gotten so specially made to match Polly's own but all the possible shades of grey and gleaming white, snow fields clean carved even in the distance under high overcast, the equally clean clouds above missing only the sharp edges, the little spaces that made pattern and texture speak of solidity, with the make-up on Mother's face a simplified diagram of how light moved on the mountain, the purple blue in the hollows, the green where hollows moved into relief just like the eye-shadow about Mother's eyes, purple in the deepest parts, green moving toward the ridges. And the clear grey blue ice of the remaining face-lifted skin pulled taut over bone just like the smoothest of the snow-fields, with the two-tone lipstick pink and then burgundy seeming stuck on, like the ski-suits of the other hotel guests scattered about them, except that Mother's mouth did not move from place to place, it only contorted itself in moans and cries, though it focused vision like the motions of those glints of harder colour against the greys and whites, against the pale blue or yellow or pink refraction of a fuller spectrum in those places where the sun shone through holes in the clouds, glinting off ice crystals that looked just like the glints off some sort of glitter on the almost invisible hairs on Mother's upper lip, a different pink to blue spreading where the only slightly nicotine yellowed teeth bite her lower one to make Polly sure that none of those other guests would wish to get this message either.

Though maybe they do, maybe there is someone out there in intense pain or concentration receiving exactly this same one, as they complete their ever more dangerous or dramatic turns, their ever continuing circles, straight up on the lifts then down in curves, over and over, shouting to each other but alone, it makes it hard to know, what they think or how much pain they are in, if threats are left at their hotel rooms if they receive the messages through their Walkmans through their cellular phones through their earmuffs or their toques or their sinuses or their teeth or their electrically wired heated ski boots that they turn on each time they get on the lifts listening to the messages or the poems as they ski, or tumbling and tumbling until legs or arms or backs or skulls shatter and break crashing into each other or trees, the messages louder and louder and faster and faster until the last moment, all of it so hard to know, if maybe the messages are left in the sauna or the pool or the bar. To make Polly wonder not for the first time or the last, why she and Mother have come here, as she watches yet a third level of colour, the sky's nuances reflected in the water of the tears in Mother's eyes, the saliva at the corner of her lips, the way Polly has seen the sky for days, refractions and reflections in or through something, glass or a mirror, water or ice, again and again, in the lodge or in the trees or in the bathroom or halfway up the mountain as she sipped the hot mulled wine Mother always allowed her when Father wasn't there, even if she shouldn't, because it seemed so continental, the way the girls at her school always talked of drinking, at least a little at home, only it didn't really work, wine out of styro-foam cups while surrounded by crowds, the boys looking at her and her looking out the window catching their reflections, or the reflection of the sky out the other side as someone walked behind her to sit down, to make her stop eating for a moment to try to focus herself in all that space as the edge of a memory would make her food suddenly unsatisfying, so that she would stop eating, say: No, I really don't like this even if she can't remember now what it was on her plate as she looks at Mother, just remembering that there hadn't been a call from Father last night, her voice never repeated that: Yes Father I'm having a wonderful time. Which Polly is sure has no connection with this, Father's failure to phone couldn't have to do with how Mother mutters something about going on: This can't go on or I can't go on, maybe meaning Father's work or the War, not her pain, or maybe it's both, maybe they're related. A thought to increase how much Polly feels herself her Mother such easy targets against the vastness, that is why the sky has been bothering her she is sure, they are so high up and so visible, no memory of a phone call but the words going on and on in her mind like the fields of snow, repeating and repeating while she tries to admire the view just like the Walrus suggested, or maybe Father had, it is just lovely the way Mother says, so that Polly has been admiring it for days, reciting those words to make it cute, to put it on the postcard, to stop it from frightening her, all that clear immensity, it's been so long since she's been out in an open space like this, which makes her try to get used to it by forcing her eyes over it again and again. The lodge at the bottom just there nestled among the trees, herself here halfway down where the trees begin, the clouds moving as the sun comes and goes, herself coming and going too, up on the lifts then slowly snaking down, so that she knows that she can change it all just by moving through it, only never enough never enough. Any more than she can change Mother's pain by letting her gaze move over the planes of the grey face as if skiing on it, change the sounds in the empty house by moving through its rooms, even stop remembering the house by being here repeating and repeating her actions, because it's only the view that changes, never the world, maybe Father can change the world with his ad campaigns, make soldiers or Oysters or clean up volunteers follow or stay behind, but she can't, the changes she can make are just in decoration, like her mother's, the giggling or yawning shifts in the direction of the conversation the new paintings on the walls the new herbs for the garden, she can help Mother select them and plant them but she can't stop Mother's pain, she can't even forget the poem, much less Cassie, even sure as she is that it was Cassie who emptied the house, the way Cassie acted.

And not the threats. That Cassie told her about. Whispering stories about how the threats caused the looks between Mother and Father, the way they spoke so low, there were threats in the mysterious phone calls, the letters without return addresses, the notes she had seen Mother looking at as she stood by the window suddenly so still. Only Cassie wouldn't tell Polly what they said or where they came from or who. Or even if they would stop she just told her to memorize that poem: Learn it, Polly, learn it, Cassie said: You'll need it to show them you know what's going on, to let them know whose side you're on, so that Polly was sure it must be that way Cassie acted and laughed which had emptied the house which had emptied her out of the house to that school deep among the trees, at least so much more sheltered than here on the mountain, she had felt safe there, listening to the girls talking about doing it or failing to do it even if she had never seen any boys not the whole time she was there, just the pictures they all pulled out and the postcards from exotic places, she will write one tonight she tells herself, to Father or one of the girls: Having a wonderful time, the snow is white as white could be, the sky is blue as blue, the reflections burn the eyes, I need new sunglasses

I've seen the most beautiful pairs, the food is good I am eating well, the people are wide-eyed and cheerful, words to feel safer by, not so exposed, Cassie should have warned her about the messages here, how Mother would get more of them, with the reception so good, no wonder she finds herself saying the poem again and again, even out loud, what she doesn't understand is why she should have to come here, why she couldn't just wait for Cassie to come home, even if Father had taken her face between his hands and said he was afraid for her, not in so many words, he just looked from her to Mother as he said he was afraid for his wife, the delicacy of her health, that was how he put it: Your Mother's health is so delicate now that Cassie is gone, and the house echoes, he said that too: the delicacy of Mother's health and the house echoes without Cassie, he said: The house echoes and I am at work so much and there are more hardships now, all of it said without mentioning the War, he never mentioned the War, just that they all had to work hard: We all have to work hard now, he said, we have to pull together, the same words used in the ads that made her say: Because of the War? only when she did he would just focus his eyes on her as if coming back from a distance and say: What war? before he would shake his head still distracted: No, no, it wasn't that, there were new ads to design. New explanations to be made.

Of how the world works she would find herself thinking, in just those words, Cassie's words, so that she would catch herself before saying them, scared suddenly that maybe Mother and Father were right, and maybe they were too late, maybe it was catching and she'd already caught it, whatever it was Cassie had, and she would bite her lips the way Mother was biting hers now. Only she never bit hers till they bled, even while Father went on his eyes once more focused behind her or in front of her but never on her face much less her eyes about the new explanations to be made and Mother alone too much: We thought you two should take a vacation together, he said, a wonderful little resort far away from it all, at the very top of the world in Canada he put it: And you both love skiing, you could join Mother for the season, it sounded like the whole season, that she wouldn't go back to school after the holidays, she would stay here until spring, until the snow melted and there were mountain goats: You're so good in school you probably won't have to lose the year and Mother needs you.

Only now Polly thinks it would have been better scuba diving. Sheltered among the seaweed coddled by the ocean, they would have been so much harder to find even if it would have been harder to eat, to have to watch all those sea creatures before you ate them, the way Mother ordered live lobster and then she and Cassie played with them in the bathtub before they were boiled, like that old joke about cannibal children being told not to play with their food, so that Cassie even gave them names while Polly could hardly manage to eat them after, it was too much like eating all the inhabitants of Mother's aquarium, and it would be worse swimming around with your tank surrounded by your food just like a shark, so that maybe it was better here after all, the stews the meat so well disguised, if it was meat at all and not synthetic the way Cassie said: Because there isn't any meat left, she would whisper, any more than oysters at the end of the poem, those words echoing as if coming from far away, the way they did in the empty house when it was only she and Cassie, Polly and Cassie, when the guests had left and there were just the words echoing, while Polly wondered if the guests weren't there any more because of Cassie, because Father and Mother didn't want to strain Cassie. Or if it was the threats they never mentioned, the way they looked at each other and said: Another one, it's hard not knowing, only Polly never heard the rest, if it was why the threats or where they were coming from or just how many guests would be at dinner, if there had been a cancellation over the phone or the latest note was just another hand written card declining an invitation, so that she asked: Is it the War? Is the General not coming any more because of the War? while Mother and Father looked at each other again, that secret indulgent look before they patted her on the head and said: War, what War? there is no War. Only then when she would say: But why does the General always talk about the War? they would say: Oh that War there's always a War. And then add, finally looking at her and smiling: But you don't have to worry about any War they're all so far away.

To make her think again Cassie surely it was Cassie all those words at the table that poem spoken again and again, that was what had emptied the house made it echo made no answer come to all her Mother's calls, made her wander its halls alone while Mother stayed later and later in bed, that was why those people were refusing the invitations, they weren't gone, surely not, those people were feasters not feasted upon, they made up the explanations they didn't have to believe them, they wouldn't follow anyone to be eaten she was quite sure of it, they were too hungry always hungry even Father always looked hungry, as if they could eat the table as well as each other as they talked. With their details of the War, their speculations on how the next campaign would go, the diffident designers of difficulties if not disasters Cassie had once called them in a moment of inspiration, just like that, out loud and pointing her fork: You Diffident Designers of Disastrous Difficulties, while she played with the lobster shells on her plate, she would always eat the lobsters while she called them by name: This is

Brainless Bobby she would say reaching the claw out to try to shake it with someone's hand, then: Goodbye Bobby's claw she would say splitting it up and swallowing it down, although soon the game was over just like the lobster and it was the Engineer Cassie seemed to be pointing at, he was so round and full to match his very round and filled out wife, just like Tweedledum and Tweedledee who recited the poem the first time, saying it to Alice, so that sometimes Polly couldn't tell if it was the Engineer speaking of disasters or difficulties or battles to be fought situations to be cleared up with Father, or if it was the wife speaking to Mother of maids and meals and details of housekeeping: It is so hard to get good help good men good meals these days but we will soon be mopping up or cleaning out, washing down or pitching in, when it wasn't just turning on or off, in or out, up or down, full of phrases like good as new when it wasn't good as gold, so that Polly would get all confused thinking that maybe it was just another ad, maybe it was all an ad maybe they just said those things to mobilize people, that was one of Father's expressions: We have to Mobilize the People. Maybe it was like in times of war, like in times of disaster, not in times of war and disaster, maybe there were no reactors exploding toxic waste seeping people killing, maybe none of the things Cassie said were true, maybe she didn't need the poem, maybe everything was too far away. And Cassie's words, Cassie's mad words, were the only reason the General didn't come any more even if Mother did come into Polly's room sometimes late at night to tell her how sorry she was, how difficult it must be, how terrible, to have to grow up in the middle of a War. And pressed her hands to Polly's hair, and Polly knew she was thinking of Cassie, how terrible it had been for Cassie even if they kept telling her how far away the War was how terribly far away. So that Polly was sure that Cassie had found something out, maybe something more than about the threats, which were after all only words, just like Cassie's.

Or that little ditty or the threats she had seen a million times on TV, black-dressed terrorist adventures and kidnappings where the man with the best weapon always won, words making up a world that didn't have to be real at all, all that sun shining at night and the shoed oysters, so that nothing Cassie said had to be true either, not even the part about the birds not flying any more, even by the sea, that was too much like the poem and not the way it was in all those picture books those TV documentaries Polly had grown up with, the ones that claimed to be true to show true pictures which Cassie said maybe they had once but not any more there weren't even any seagulls and *they* lived on garbage. And it was the case that Polly hadn't seen any, not outside the aviaries at school or the country club or the one Mother kept, certainly there are none here, the only bright movement is the ski-suits, but maybe it's always like that in the mountains in winter, Polly doesn't know, though there had been plenty of birds that summer she had gone with her parents to that other country nestled among its own mountains, where the people wore hats like the toques here, only brighter, the colours more jangling like the blue of that sky, she looks but can't find any colours as bright, even as the sun peeks out a moment, it's her and Mother's turn now for the spot of sun, just a brief glow for one moment here at the very edge of the tree line, the tree right below them gleaming a brighter green for just an instant, the edge of Mother's ski making its one metallic flash, that can be seen for miles Polly is sure, and trembles again at this total exposure while Mother massages her foot: You have no idea how much it hurts Polly, oh god you couldn't know, any more than she could understand why they were here, always on top of things, what Cassie had complained about in that country with the hats, all that travel by helicopter: Some overview she had said: We always look down. To pick up the local colour Father had explained, talking about the ad campaign he was working on then, for travel or for the products of national culture Polly wasn't sure, for the new military government Cassie whispered later: First they bomb it then they advertise it, much later and very quietly, even Cassie wouldn't say that at table, so that Polly was left not knowing what to believe, Cassie or the posters for a new beauty product that was somehow more beautiful with the mountains behind and those bright coloured costumes, they all agreed on the local colour and she did remember how the models leapt out of the helicopters to pose, the natives sitting at their feet in their colours, though she wasn't altogether sure she had the right place, there had been at least one other mountainous country, where the colours were bright too, but the patterns smaller and more complex, and the models with purple lips and violet eyes.

Maybe models just went with mountains, all of them white like snow with just a few freckles showing through the make-up, but never any wrinkles like Mother had around the eyes even in the same make-up for when the sun is bright, maybe that was all it was, a worldwide campaign for Mountain Make-up, specially formulated against the harsh reflections or the rays that shone through the fleeing ozone layer, Polly doesn't know if that's Cassie speaking again or part of the advertising, is it the ad men frightening everyone into wearing more make-up or just Cassie whispering: That's why they do it, you know, that's why, they wear all that stuff, it's not for beauty at all. And it's true that Mother even covers the thick violet around her eyes with those bright yellow sunglasses that everyone seems to have, bright yellow or purple or magenta or green, along with those funny little flat caps where the visor and the crown snap together as if everyone were driving along back country roads, all part of the best equipment to meet the ultimate challenge, that's what all the brochures said: Come for the ultimate adventure of Man against the Mountain, or was it in Man against the Mountain, that might be a question for one of her teachers, 'in' or 'of' if you're against the mountain, with so much blue on the pamphlets Mother had sent her, so much blue in the five colour separation, when Mother wanted to persuade her to come on this vacation of her own free will, only it just made her want more green more brown more shelter, so that Polly had almost mentioned it, how there must still be places like that around, the school couldn't be the only one, where the girls just giggled about Man against the Mountain, they didn't take it seriously at all, maybe they were too used to being tucked away where no messages could get through, at least Polly thought they couldn't, and didn't care about anything, not even the War, only when she said that, one of them had to explain: It's not about the War, silly. It's not about combat training, it isn't Man at war with the mountain, or people in the mountains, it was just the challenge of it, skiing was so much fun, the costumes and the boys, so that she'd understood suddenly, while another one of the girls talked about all those gorgeous hunks against the mountain, posing in their ski-suits, which made her see them suddenly, all those models against the mountain from that other trip, and she wondered if maybe this was part of another ad campaign, maybe Father had invented it, that Man against the Mountain, it sounded so much like dinner conversation, and this was another one of his freebies, the way they had gotten that other free trip that had turned out so badly, only it was woman against the mountain there, up against the mountain with the blue behind and those people with those hats over their ears and the wooden flutes and cane panpipes somewhere down around the women's knees and all of it beautiful like here. Only greener as you looked down even if it was so high that Polly can remember one of the women taking a hit from an oxygen bottle, while all of them drank the coca water, the camera crew and the models and the make-up artists and her parents drinking away as the natives chewed the leaves only they wouldn't give it to her or even to Cassie: We don't want any bad habits starting Mother said with her tightest smile while Polly remembered what happened when she and Cassie were in bed, it was part of entertaining, having drugs around, the refined kind they must have here on the mountain too, as white as snow, maybe something like that could protect Mother from the messages, she used to take something to stop them from getting in, stop her feeling the pain, even if it slurred her speech, but Polly wouldn't even know where to ask. Cassie would have known but she was gone, after warning Polly about what would happen, after the messages had started on that trip when they kept having to leave in the helicopters, no one would say why, just: We have to move out fast, packing up the models and the equipment and sometimes a panpipe or two maybe a flute or a hat, leaving the natives there until one day Cassie didn't just giggle and speak of overviews through tight lips. She started screaming.

Why do we keep doing this she screamed over and over: WHY, WHY WHY are we always on top of things, why don't we ever know what's really going on, why do we always take something away but never someone, why don't they ever come with us why don't we speak to them, why do we just leave them here to die, they all die you know they all do THEY DIE, THEY DIE, I can feel them, you know that, I can feel them I CAN FEEL THEM DIE, why can't you feel it WHY CAN'T YOU, she had howled. And then she had disappeared, for three weeks she had disappeared: I'm going for a walk she said: A long walk, she had written in the note she had left, even if it was nowhere near the sea, and then she had added something about talking of many things, though she never did mention with whom, whose story she planned to listen to or whose explanation, or even how she expected to find it, if she could find anyone. Because by the end of the trip there hadn't even been any more hikers coming through. Although it was obvious when Cassie was found, by one of the helicopters, wandering in a deserted village square holding a set of panpipes in her hands, that she had completely changed.

She just looked at them with those accusing eyes and she never screamed any more just recited in that same high singsong in which she had first recited the poem back when she and Polly were still little girls: we just come in and eat their food and take their pictures we even get the recipes to send them home telling people their stories as if they were still there, STILL THERE, STILL THERE, her voice suddenly raucous and cawing like a crow: STILL THERE STILL THERE, THEY'RE NOT THEY'RE NOT, repeating it and repeating it until her hoarse voice lowered to an intense monotone whisper as she pointed her fork across the table, with the orange and yellow-black body of the mussel still on it: There are just those pretty pictures in the living room these dishes you tell the maid to make, to be put on walls or kept on tables or shelves or melted in our mouths, her voice slowly rising again with the rhythm of the words until it was once more the rising and falling pattern of childhood poetry recitals: Where we can take them out and look at them to say how good they taste how fine they are even pick them up we bring things back hats and flutes that Polly plays while someone listens and says how pretty how pretty when we know very well that they have been consumed CONSUMED CONSUMED, the war has consumed them, IT HAS IT HAS we've eaten them all up YOU HAVE YOU HAVE YOU YOU she would scream across the table at Father: YOU, spitting or foaming at the mouth until she would start to giggle: you can't have your cake and eat it too, repeating it over and over the words all jumbled: YOUR CAKE AND EAT IT YOU CAN'T HAVE NOT TOO NOT TOO NOT CAKE AND EAT YOU CAN'T AND TOO NOT YOU NOT YOU, until the syllables ran together and it was just noise: nottooeeeat-cancakeyoucakeyou tooeettooeeeeattooeeet and she took whatever half chewed mess she had in her mouth and addressed herself to it: HAVE YOU AND EAT TOO, the tears running out of her eyes while she took deep hiccoughing breaths just long enough to steady herself so that she could start to talk again: WHAT WHAT those pictures and those recipes and all those lovely things as if they might be sealing wax or kings because we know that something's boiling hot and all your pigs have wings AND FLY AND FLY AND BOMB AND BOMB so that even the sea is boiling hot with radio-activity she would say and throw the shells: The birds will eat them THE BIRDS THE BIRDS your birds Mother YOURS YOURS you have the last of them YOU KNOW YOU KNOW only the pigs have wings now, only the General's pigs, and her voice would be a whisper again, or a caw, a terrible hollow raucous laugh and it didn't matter who was there it just went on and on until Father would finally make the decision to remove her from the table, forcibly if necessary. Only to find her in her room later repeating the words of the poem without either looking at him or stopping, just reciting it over and over like saying prayers on a rosary or the mantra of some strange new religion going on for hours or even days. Which was when the messages had become more frequent. At least that's what Cassie said made it so usual to watch Mother holding some part of her body and moaning, Polly had observed that Cassie was right about that.

So it was no surprise that Mother had needed to get away once Cassie disappeared. Melted back into that smog-bound city where neither Polly nor Mother had been by themselves in years, they stayed in a glass encased world, framed by car windows and restaurant windows and house windows, by plants and animals and birds, on this not that side, the outer gardens were gravel and iron, sand and wood, still water and steel, all post-modern Mother called it, though Polly didn't know if she meant the architecture that surrounded them, or the lives they lived inside all that glass with all the vents and colour-coded tubes needed to process the air and water maintain the even heat, all left visible to please the eye and to show how the building worked, it was very fashionable to show how buildings worked, to turn them inside out or skin them like an anatomy diagram to show the veins and arteries: You can show how anything works just as long as it's not the world, Cassie would say: Anything. Father's ad campaigns through from beginning photograph to finished five colour separation, make-up being put on the model's face, the model posing up against the mountain, just as long as they didn't know where the ideas were coming from or why or where the people were going or why the building needed that special venting system, because you could see the mechanics but never the reason: How they eat each other YUMM, gobble each other YUMM, how there's hardly anything left YUMM, as long as you don't see that YUMM, while Polly would try not to listen, to just sit back and enjoy it all, it was pretty, models with multi-coloured make-up to match the woven hats or the painted metal constructions of the ski-lifts below her or even the pipes in subtle colours crawling across the ceilings of the country club where Mother would take them which wasn't so much country any more even if the best families still went there, at least that's what Mother said: The best families still come here, but an enclosed space with horses and riding trails and trees and jogging ovals and tennis courts and pools with waves that imitated the ocean even if the smell was of chlorine instead of salt spray so that you couldn't smell anything, not the horse manure or the flowers or the food you were served under little beach umbrellas which didn't matter much since it all probably tasted the same anyway which was probably good and Mother said the beach was much too dirty: Oh, Polly, you don't want to go there, she said, and admired the post-modern architecture instead: It's so lovely.

While Polly snuck looks at the waiters in their skimpy bathing trunks and their artificial tans with their bulges that might be artificial too as she would giggle and take the long drinks they brought in coconuts and pineapples, alcoholic for Mother: Virgin for the virgin, the waiter would whisper to her and wink, so that she giggled again and enjoyed herself even if she did wish for the places in the tropics they had once gone, or the places like this one they could still come, the carefully painted pipes of its lifts, scattered over the mountain so that she wondered if maybe this wasn't post-modern too, though she couldn't figure how it might explain the workings of the mountain, maybe it just pointed out man working against the mountain, maybe those fine cables and bright towers and complicated snow-making equipment, on special days spraying out pastel coloured snow, were the much advertised Ultimate Adventure in Man against the Mountain, because maybe that's what post-modern did mean after all, the lifts were just man framing the mountain the way some of the girls at school, the arts majors just making their plans to go on to major universities, that's what they talked about, the importance of the frame in the post-modern, the framing device, the lifts certainly qualified as a device, as they tried to figure out whether post-modern was a way to frame the natural or the primitive, or even the modern, that had a few adherents, to separate the natural from the man-made, to not get your signals, or maybe it was your signs, crossed, or some such, those were the ones who thought Father was in a *thrilling* line of work: You could use all your semiology, they said, making Polly want to tell them Father wasn't seamy at all, while they went on, all talking just the same way Mother did, Mother even brought it up with Cassie, as they flew back from that deserted village in the helicopter: Isn't it beautiful, Cassie, she said, looking down on the outlines of fields cultivated for hundreds of years by the natives of those parts, until very recently: It's so post-modern. And she touched the edge of the helicopter door with her hand: See how technology frames the primitive landscape, it's so like Father's collection, the way Mother had often remarked on things with Cassie, Cassie had always been the artistic one, and Polly supposed Mother was right, and almost said so, they did seem to need the door of the copter and the pattern of its flight to make a frame that could bring into focus this other world and make it belong to them just the way the developed pictures did, only she never got the time to say it, Cassie, still all dirty and obviously tired, just turned on Mother and started to scream, so that Polly thought at first it was just the terrible ordeal Cassie must have been through, maybe she'd been kidnapped, nothing to do with Mother at all, because Cassie laughed too, and even hiccoughed. Only soon Polly heard the words: FRAME, FRAME, FRAME, she heard: That's right frame, we are a frame, just like the bombsights, they are a frame. We frame the primitive so the bombs can swallow it, SHAME SHAME SHAME, they swallow the primitive and the primitives too, the bombs swallow them, FRAME FRAME FRAME SHAME SHAME SHAME, FRAME SHAME, SHAME FRAME SHAME SHAME SHAME, you don't see any people down there Mother do you? because we fly above it all, us and the bombers, till there's nobody left. SHAME SHAME SHAME.

The way Father had said that often enough when Cassie had first started asking all her questions and being so worried: Don't worry we're above all that, just the way Polly and Mother really are above all that here at the juncture of two watersheds no matter what Cassie said with her gestures like for the "Itsy Bitsy Spider" when you say "the rain came down and washed the spider out," that no one could be above it all, could they? not if the pollution was above all of them. And it came raining down even on the pure white snow, Cassie was convinced that's why you shouldn't eat it, it had nothing to do with the danger of hypothermia: That's just what they tell you Polly, it's poisonous is all, and the ozone layer that was supposed to be above that, it was almost gone, so you had to wear all the bright new ultra-protection ski make-up just like Father's ads against the mountain said, only it would never be enough, there would never be enough protection, not with the messages: No one can be above it all any more Cassie had said in her new hoarse whisper: Not even us, so that she had even said it to Father that last time he had patted her, rubbing the young flesh like a good luck charm, telling her she didn't need the make-up yet that she was above all that, saying it again the way he had always said: Of course we're above it all. You're above all that.

Only this time she had just broken from his grip and turned around and laughed her high pitched laugh then whispered: But what is there to be above if there is no one there?

And when Father had tried to put his hand back on her shoulder and say: Oh Cassie, Cassie, she had started to recite the poem, only to stop in the middle and say: Don't you think I know you've eaten them? Don't you think I know? How well you've prepared them with salt and bread and words while Father just stared at her, his hand still above her shoulder as she went on, singsong again: You've *ea*ten the *Ge*neral and sw*a*llowed the *E*ngineer, slurp-slurp, slurp-slurp, she said: You've *ea*ten them, slurp-slurp I watched, slurp-slurp I saw, slurp-slurp how you sl*u*rped them up, slurp-slurp how you sw*a*llowed them down, while Father shrugged: It has nothing to do with me, placing his hands behind his back his voice gone sweet: That's not the kind of work I do, you know that Cassie, it isn't my fault, and his voice was clipped now, like the voices in the ads, sweet but clipped, the voice of authority speaking to someone too dumb to understand but nice anyway, someone he was sure didn't speak his language: I'm just an adman Cassie, it has nothing to do with us, with this family or with the Agency, that his government has fallen that he didn't know how to conduct his War, that the latest ad campaign we were asked to do was against him, that has nothing to do with me, you know we're above all that, you're above all that, repeating it again and again, like a hypnosis tape that could in itself convince her, until he shrugged once more, and Polly heard a slight trembling note of humour: Besides, as you know very well, it's all the same, and here Polly couldn't tell if he said: To us which General governs, or: Which General governs us, with the way Cassie shouted, her voice her own again for just one moment: Don't try that shit with me, the time that has come to talk of many things, I'm older than the oldest oyster now, and I won't go for a walk either, I won't even listen, and she'd stuck her fingers in her ears: To any more of that shit, because there's only one thing left to talk about, there has only been one thing to talk about for the longest time, and that's WHAT'S ON THE MENU, what the hell you're going to do when YOU'VE EATEN THEM ALL, her hissing whisper echoing through the house: Who the hell will you tell your stories to then?

While Cassie laughed and kept on laughing, even when Father raised his hand to strike her, something he had never done, he had never hit either of them. And she had skipped down the hall scampering from side to side her laughter echoing as he screamed after her his hand still raised: OUT OUT, I will have you sent away I WILL I WILL, I am tired of your MAD INFLUENCE on the peace of this house, I am tired of your MAD INFLUENCE on this family, you don't appreciate anything, you don't care what it's cost us to keep you comfortable, you don't even care about Mother, about all she's done for you, why can't you see what you're doing to her health? and then he had answered himself: Because you're MAD Cassie MAD, you hear me MAD, MAD MAD CASSIE, you don't understand anything, as his voice suddenly softened and he shook his head to say: And I am very sorry. Very very sorry. But we will have to put you somewhere MAD people go. Oh, Cassie, I am sorry it has come to this, as Cassie just shouted back, over the sound of the door slamming: YOU CAN'T EAT ME, you can't you can't YOU WON'T YOU WON'T nobody's going to eat me I'VE GOTTEN THE MESSAGE, nya-nya nya-nya-nya. And then the next thing Polly knew the words to the poem came blaring out over the in-house intercom.

And then that night Cassie had come to visit Polly in her room to say goodbye, and to try, at least that's what she said, to explain. How Polly had to understand about the messages. About the poem and the messages. And even if Polly hadn't believed a word Cassie said, her last words nonetheless re-enter Polly's mind as she watches Mother writhing in that pain that has over the years become worse and worse until it's left her wiggling back and forth in the snow as if she was trying to bury herself the way a clam might in the sand

["For some of us are out of breath,
And all of us are fat!"]

or an oyster trying to get away from the Walrus and his lemon, wiggling and wiggling, her face such a terrible gray, while Cassie's words speak themselves and Polly can't hold the poem off any more, it's back, and Cassie's voice, too, it's a stereo set with two different tracks, with the words exactly as Cassie had spoken them just before she took Polly's old cast metal antique clown lamp and smashed the window in her room all the way through its three layers of glass, to climb through the hole. While Polly, unused to the smog in the air, at least she thought that's what the acrid smell was, it wasn't her own fear, had fallen down on her floor and hovered for hours on the verge of consciousness.

Only to have Mother tell her: The smog is hardly that bad, Polly, I mean it's nice to have the air filter, it does make the air smell better but it's hardly necessary, there's no reason to get scared and hysterical over a little smog, Polly, I'm sorry Cassie did this to you, made you listen to all her stories, but it's not deadly the way Cassie said you know, and she had caressed Polly's head and brought her special tea made from the herbs in the conservatory, and Mother had told her a bedtime story just the way she had when both sisters were much younger, while letting Polly sleep in her bedroom until Polly's own was fixed, and then after that Polly had been sent away to school. Never to tell Mother what Cassie had said. Even during the evenings when she watched Mother double over with pain before taking her pills. Largely because Polly had herself forgotten as she listened to everyone talk about how hard it was on Mother that Cassie had run away like that,

> **["'No hurry!' said the Carpenter,**
> **They thanked him much for that."]**

and how terribly sick Cassie was, so that Polly could decide that was all it had ever been, a madness, a terrible madness, just like Father said, as she slowly erased those last words from her mind. Cassie's explanation of how the world worked, her terrible fantasy world, absent from Polly's mind until now. When she hears, vaguely disembodied as though transmitted over great distances, not just the poem, it's not just the poem re-entering, though soon she will wish it were as she listens to that same disembodied desperate voice, so like Cassie's voice, repeating this time not simply the story of the poor oysters' fate, but the words, the exact words, now clear again and precise, that Cassie had spoken that final night. Exactly.

Polly is sure.

> **<<Death Threats, Death Threats, listen to her ask, are they death threats, poor little Polly, are they death threats? Well what do you think? Are they death threats, death threats death threats everything's a**

death threat. The food the water the air is a death threat. And that's the whole point Polly,

["'A loaf of bread,' the Walrus said,
'Is what we chiefly need:"]

the Planet is tired of death threats, death threats, of our Father's death threats, the whole earth is tired Polly and She's fighting back, The Planet is fighting back.

Fighting back so that one of these days Polly you'll have to stop with your isn't he cute and isn't the house nice and wasn't the General funny did you see his face when he talked about the War, stop being like mother with her giggles and her clothes and her thinking Father will protect her, even with all her pain all her headaches all her indigestion thinking Father will protect her. Because he can't he won't he doesn't even want to and pretty soon if you're not careful you'll start getting them too, if you don't wise up and join the right side, you'll start receiving the Messages so the least you can do is learn this poem to prove you understand,

["Pepper and vinegar besides
Are very good indeed—"]

because I won't be here to help you, I'm going to join the few that are left because they need me the Planet needs me She needs us and I'll go do what I can because the PLANET IS DYING, Polly, the whole Planet and She needs our help,

["Now, if you're ready, Oysters dear,
We can begin to feed.'"]

THE PLANET IS DYING and I can feel it, I CAN FEEL IT, just the way Mother can Polly every time a child is born without arms or legs she scratches the spot every time someone starves to death her stomach shrinks every time a woman is beaten she holds her head, every time someone's toenails or fingernails are pulled out she grabs her hand her foot her elbow and screams only it's not what she says not indigestion or migraine or arthritis or rheumatism or whiplash or MS or PMS it's all the tortured and the dying

["'But not on us!' the Oysters cried,
Turning a little blue."]

it's all of them Polly all the ones that are left and even if she won't admit it Polly she told me. Told me how it is, how soon Father will have no one left to eat, she didn't mean to but she did. Looking at those natives carrying terrible burdens up those mountains, you must remember them Polly, you must remember how you looked at them and said poor things burdens bigger than they were being carried up the mountains with ropes around their foreheads they say that's the only way a person can carry more than their weight and you there watching so decrepit they looked so deformed by the pollution only you thought it was just the weight, they used to carry people up the mountains like that, people like the General or the Engineer,

["'After such kindness, that would be
A dismal thing to do!'"]

and you Polly, oh the poor things the poor things and Mother turning your head away, shush poor Polly, you don't understand poor Polly, they don't feel it the way we do poor Polly, that's what she said.

And that's how she told me that she knows even if she won't admit it, because they don't Polly, you know that they don't, they don't feel it the way we do at all they don't, she's right, she's right, but not why you might think, or the girls at the Country Club. Not because they're used to it but because THE PLANET PROTECTS THEM. When things get really bad, the Planet protects them, She takes all that pain and all that suffering away from them Polly so that they won't feel it any more so that they can at least die in peace even if they've never lived in peace so that when it's too fantastically bad it's not just the coca leaves or the water or the heroin that protects them it's the Planet Polly and they don't feel it any more at all, only it's not easy Polly you know that even for the Planet it's not because there's a law of the Conservation of Energy you must remember from school Newton's second law or maybe it's his first but it's very important no energy can be created or destroyed it can only be transferred well pain is the same way pain is energy, it's the first law of psycho-dynamics, pain can be created but not destroyed not even the planet can make it go away, She can only transfer it or confer it,

["'The night is fine,' the Walrus said.
'Do you admire the view?'"]

and She confers it on Mother and you needn't look at me with such surprise Polly Pretty Polly with your little round mouth Polly Pretty Polly your how could anyone do that to Mother mouth, Polly Pretty Polly your Mother is such a good person mouth, your Cassie you must be mistaken mouth, well don't bother saying it, OK, because I know what I'm talking about,

["'It was so kind of you to come!
And you are very nice!'"]

I'm telling you Mother may not be Father she may not be the Walrus charming the poor little Oysters into following her, telling them how nice they are telling them to take their minds off things to make them aid in their own destruction maybe she isn't like that but have you ever known her to stop eating Polly to say anything but the butter's spread too thick or cut me another slice have you Polly have you,

["The Carpenter said nothing but
'Cut us another slice."]

she may not trick them but she certainly eats them have you ever known her to stop eating Polly have you, you know you haven't, to stop eating or asking for butter, or white wine sauce, or a little more paprika while she eats down to the last nibble all the little shells and the gristle and the hair and the fingernails her own fingernails while she manages the conversation with her small comments,

["I wish you were not quite so deaf—
I've had to ask you twice!'"]

she's such a good Carpenter better than the one in the poem and not just with a hammer, in the conversation too always fixing things if the General's son is allergic to oysters she gets him mussels if the conversation strains the Engineer's wife she changes the subject, all the cutting and fixing the measuring of food and words don't kid yourself Polly she's making each person fit, dovetailing the joints sanding down the concepts cementing the parts together with the epoxy of all those ooohs and aahs and oh yeses and oh dears and how marvelouses and isn't that awfuls and all the rest as she twists her fork into the shell all mother of pearl to match her make-up

["It seems a shame,' the Walrus said,
'To play them such a trick."]

twisting with her fork to dislodge the animal pluck and slurp you remember how she looks when she does it Polly, she deserves exactly what she gets, even when she suddenly lets her fork drop and that expression comes across her face, or she screams in her room.

I understand. And even if Father even if the General, whichever General is left, even if they kill me or they eat me the way they do in some places after they decontaminate the meat, or they just use me up, whatever they may do to me, no one who's being eaten being tortured being used up, will ever have to send a message to me the way they do to Mother,

["After we've brought them out so far,
And made them trot so quick!'"]

because I already understand now and I'm going to see if we can't get the message through to the General to the Engineer to the Doctor, even to Father, difficult as that may be since he isn't sensitive to anything but his own appetite not the way Mother is no matter what Father says about how he sympathizes with the plight of the poor or the war-struck or the famine starved or the plague ridden or the pollution deformed he doesn't he just thinks about some other story to tell the ones that are left to make them believe in him,

["The Carpenter said nothing but
'The butter's spread too thick!'"]

well maybe we'll never get through but we're sure going to try only maybe there aren't even enough of us left any more even with the Planet on our side, maybe there aren't enough left to even reach Father, if the Planet isn't quick when the tortured die the pain goes out into the atmosphere and helps to corrode the ozone, so maybe we won't be able to, maybe it's too late to reach any of them the way we do Mother, with the cries of the tortured and the dying, but we'll try we will. KILLED BUT NOT EATEN. EATEN BUT NOT DIGESTED. THESE ARE OUR MOTTOES. NEVER DIGESTED. A MESSAGE IN EVERY MOR-

SEL. LONG LIVE THE HEROIC RESISTANCE OF THE PLANET EARTH. JOIN US. JOIN US. JOIN US. JAAAAAAAJ OOOOOOO. JAAAAAAAAGH AAAAGH AAAAAAAGH AAAAGH AAAAGH. >

Only as she listens Polly is sure this is not the way Cassie's speech had ended. Especially as she watches her mother writhe in the snow: God my feet, my feet are burning,

< RRRRRRAAAAAARRRRRR ERRRRRR AAAAAAGH OOOOOOO GGGAAAAGH JOOOIN USSSSSSS GAARRRRRRR GGGOOOOOO >

["'I weep for you,' the Walrus said:
'I deeply sympathize.'"]

burning, burning hot, they're burning. While Polly is sure that as she left Cassie had never screamed. Those were Cassie's words and the voice in her mind is so much Cassie's voice, but still there had been no incoherent phrases, no slogans, no screaming. Nothing is as it should be, it just isn't right, no more right than a sun that shines at night or Mother, claiming to be burning hot in the ice cold and smearing snow into her hair as she turns her twisted face toward Polly: Oh my head my head my feet god my feet my hand my arm right there in the first joint oh god my teeth my teeth they're being pulled out of my head, on and on in rhythm to the screams a new combined poem

< AAAAAAAAAAGH AAAAAAAAAGH GAAAAAGH GAAAAGH JOIN US JOIN US AAAAAAAAAAGH GAAGH GAGH AAGHH >

["With sobs and tears he sorted out
Those of the largest size,"]

inside Polly's head the way maybe the Carpenter's feet burning on the sand knew what the Carpenter didn't, Mother's body does know what Mother has refused to acknowledge, all that history of digestion and pain behind her gentlest words, all the terror in her now blind eyes, the ones that look right through Polly as she screams again, no longer: My head my hand my elbow my belly my foot, not even Polly's own name but: Cassie, Cassie, Cassie. Cassie please. Please please, over and over to make tears come to Polly's eyes now, unsure for a moment if Mother misses Cassie, how much she must miss Cassie

["Holding his pocket-handkerchief
Before his streaming eyes."]

<JOIAAAAGH GAAAAAGU UUUSSSAGH GAARRRR ARRR URRR GAAAAAAGH AAAAAAAGH GAAAAGH GOOOOOOOOOOOOOO AA >

Polly trying to tell herself that it's love and worry and the hurt of betrayal that brings Cassie's name to Mother's lips, that brings this on only the screaming in her head won't allow her to let go of what she already knows to be true as Mother says, her body almost buried in the snow: No Cassie, no, don't let it happen to you, Cassie no,

["'O Oysters,' said the Carpenter,
'You've had a pleasant run!"]

<GGAGH AAAAACH RESISTTTTTTT AAAAGH GARRR ARRR HELLLLP THE PLAAAAAANET AAAAAAAGH GAAAAAGH AAA >

don't let them do it, stop it. Please, stop it.

Until Polly is convinced that Mother does not address her own pain, but Cassie's torturers. Because Cassie has told her the truth. It has been true all along. All those things Cassie said at table. All those things Polly had refused to remember. And the message Mother is receiving now is the news that it is Cassie's turn. The pain of Cassie dying.

So that before the ski patrol can finally arrive with its stretcher Polly panics and skis away, her skis leaving a last pastel rainbow arc behind her as she pushes off to move as fast as she can, down and down like they taught her in the race clinic,

["Shall we be trotting home again?'
But answer came there none—"]

< SSSSAAAAAAAVVE MEEEEE SAAAAVE THE PLAAAAANET AAAGH GAAAAGH AAAAAAAAAAAAAAAGGGOOOOOO AAAGHH >

turning and turning, faster and faster, down past the lifts and past the lift-lines past the lodge and along the ski-out long made obsolete by the use of helicopters. Trying to make herself believe that if she just skis far enough she will come to a road full of cars that will lead to a city full of people as bright-eyed and cheerful as the ones on the postcard she has bought, as multitudinous and various, as interesting and healthy, as the ones in Father's ad campaigns, skiing and skiing while tears stream down her face and she shouts against the wind not: Stay Cassie please, Father will help you, you need help Cassie you do, the way she did as Cassie dropped from her window, but: Oh Cassandra how could you leave me, as the poem reaches its end

> **["And this was scarcely odd, because**
> **They'd eaten every one."]**

< AAAAAGH GAAAAGHHHHHH >

as does the screaming in her head.

Though she is too far away now to hear her Mother calling out behind her: No Polly, no, not you too, before Mother is silent and silence reigns utterly in the dead white winter world Polly moves through. While somewhere far away in front of a fire Father shakes his head, and thinks surely he can't be getting a headache, he never gets headaches, surely this twinge, maybe he's been working too hard, he must try harder to get away; before eating yet another one of his oysters Rockefeller, which aren't nearly as good as they should be, it's been years since you could find really good, large oysters. Then he yawns and commands his word processor, it's a hard life but a good one, to print still another line.

Paramilitary Parafictions

* [Seven Elementary Catastrophes:
A Set of Footnotes
in search of their text]

---

1. Although she acknowledges the initiating role of his torture and the three years he subsequently spent in jail, his wife concurs in that his definitive downward spiral was set off by his inability to acquire the new language. She also reports that she cannot get through to him on any level now, even in the language they share. "He seems to think that I haven't suffered. Just because I don't have the scars on my chest from the acid the way he does. Just because I have full use of my hands. But he doesn't know what I went through the time he was in jail either. When the death squads were looking for me and I had to dress as a prostitute just to get out of the place after I visited him. You should have seen me all tarted up and with a skirt up to here, that the real whores lent me. And then once they [the death squad] followed me and I got on a bus, the number two I think but I didn't know where it went, and when I got off at the end of the line

it was a market and there was a shootout where some people died but they didn't get me and I felt so sorry but what could I do, or the time I went to visit my kids, I had them hidden by then and I had to hide inside a latrine all night. But that wasn't the worst of it, not even the smell. Because the twenty-one days he was disappeared I hunted among the corpses in the clandestine graveyards, you know about those, with my one year old on my back, I had nowhere to put her yet, and I don't know how to say it, you can't know about this, but there's a smell, so sweet, and no matter how many times you wash your clothes, you can't get rid of it."

2. **Translator's Note:** There are many figures in Salvadoran folktales that can be looked upon as weakened Pre-Columbian gods or spirits of place, much the way leprechauns and fairies are the shrunken leftovers of the pre-Christian Celtic religions. One, La Ciguanava, is a *llorona* type figure, and may well be part of the same myth system as the legendary Mexican lady of that name, since the areas in which she occurs have the same myth and language base. She stands under trees crying, her *rebozo* wrapped about her. Sometimes she will follow men or walk ahead of them. One informant reported that La Ciguanava's position ahead or behind him dictated his luck in that night's fishing. Another such figure is El Cipitin, about whom less is known. He is seen as a child of about ten years who will come into the sugar cane mills to eat the ash that is left from the process of refinement, leaving his footprints in the morning. None of the informants seemed to know more about him, or the reasons behind his strange diet.

---

3. While his problems with the new language were manifest even in his classes, where he would seem to lack concentration, spending much time staring out windows or at points in space, or objects, they were apparently much worse at home. When he attempted to do written assignments, especially journal writing, he would become very agitated, complaining of headaches, screaming at his wife and children, or even hurling the textbooks across the room. "It really isn't right, to blame me, you know," his wife says. "I had to learn to speak. I was the one who went all over the city, even into the bars, to hunt down foreign journalists to make my denunciations. I told them all about him, about how he had disappeared, about how he had been taken away, about how I couldn't find him, it was during the civilian government when they were trying to look good interna-

tionally. That's how I started my work with the Human Rights Commission. And then I really learned. All the relevant words. Disappearance, torture, corpse, mutilation, percentage. In it seemed like at least ten languages. I probably saved his life. I didn't want to show him up."

---

4. **Translator's Note:** It is interesting that even in the devastated Salvadoran countryside one can note the laws of applied linguistics at work. Just as the Spanish *peligro* (danger) derived from the Latin *periculum* through compression and consonant reversal, we can see the same process at work on the rather sophisticated and until now little-used word *bombardeo* (bombardment). This word is now commonly said *borbandeo*, achieving greater ease of pronunciation through both the consonant reversal and the opening of the 'm' into 'n' because of its proximity to the 'd.' Both the peasants who are the victims of the act it signifies and their well educated advocates now say the word in this manner. We can only speculate that the final monument to the 70,000 dead in El Salvador's ten year civil war may be the permanent passing of the word *borbandeo* into the Spanish lexicon. Or wonder what the effects of continued oral usage will be on the utterly foreign word *napalm* (napalm).

5. While it is generally acknowledged that first language acquisition quickly centres in one defined area of the left cerebral cortex, there is an increasing body of evidence to indicate that second language acquisition is more decentralized. Some part of the new lexicon may be located near the first language centre, while others may be located scattershot, even word by word, throughout the cerebral cortex. A secondary language centre may also develop in the brain's right hemisphere. It has been suggested that besides the words that exist in direct translation, transparent to the mind in both languages simultaneously, much vocabulary is segregated by language. Thus when the signifier is triggered into consciousness by direct or indirect apprehension (usually a visual image) of the signified, or at the end of a syntactical chain in one of the two languages, it still remains hidden, though known, in the other. The location of a word in left or right hemisphere may be tested through the blocking of one eye when the object is shown. It is the existence of two such parallel but unconnected lexicons that makes it possible for the authors to posit the existence of words or concepts so well hidden and powerful in

their effect on the subject, that they will sabotage those changes to personality and body language necessary to satisfactorily complete acquisition of a new target language, or even dictate a reactive blurring to the personality in the fully acquired language of which they should be a part. We are now beginning our search for these saboteurs in left and right brain, as well as in the body itself: the swollen tongue, the empty gums, the hard scarred skin, the twisted bones and unseeing eyes. We will then extend it to movement, to the mind and body at one in a tiny gesture or tone, that seems to bring on silence and the aborted moment of recall.

6. Although she has been helpful to us in many areas, his wife is uncooperative in the area of her husband's hallucinations. An educated woman acquainted with both culture shock and the concept of Post Traumatic Stress Disorder and how it can trigger long after the event, as it often does in Vietnam Veteran's Syndrome, she nonetheless says that she too was brought up to believe in ghosts, and in her country's folkloric figures. As she puts it, "Look, I grew up terrified of my dead grandmother rattling the dishes in the cupboard on the Day of the Dead just like everyone else did. And when a neighbour told me about the dog he saw as big as a pony with glowing red eyes salivating and baring his teeth down by the graveyard, well I didn't walk on that road for a long time. Still, after so many days and nights among the dead, turning the bodies over one by one, and sleeping among them with the death squad looking for me— they didn't come to haunt me. So I'm not afraid any more. But if he says they come to haunt him, or that the Ciguanava walks with him, or El Cipitin has come to Canada to play with his children's shiny plastic toys, Jesus Christ, man, he has better reason than most. And if they whisper and share a private language the rest of us don't know, well, they go back a long way. Who are we to interrupt a conversation between such old friends?"

7. Juan Pablo Letelier, son of assassinated Chilean diplomat Orlando Letelier, speaking in Calgary, April 3, 1989. "Although none of the casualties were inflicted in conflicts between nation states [but rather, in conflicts along the internal ideological frontiers imposed by the national security state], it can be said that in the last decade we have lived a third world war in South America. You know those casualties. They walk here among us."

The Deconstruction of Wesley Smithson

For Mark Murphy

b. July 31st, 1912, Monmouth, Illinois, U.S.A.

d. July 31st, 1952, Johannesberg, South Africa

on assignment

A Brief Introduction to the Final Tapes of Noted Journalist Wesley Smithson

Though much has been written to date on the disappearance of noted journalist Wesley Smithson (whose name, he always said, must not be confused with that of noted American arms manufacturer Smith and Wesson), little of that writing has done anything to clear up the mystery that surrounds the event. It is for this reason that the following tapes, sent anonymously to this paper, have been received so enthusiastically. Although the tapes offer little by way of clarifying Mr. Smithson's whereabouts or his current condition, they do offer a great deal of evidence as to his state of mind on or about the time of his disappearance.

There is no doubt in our minds that these tapes, which comprise almost all six sides of three ninety minute cassettes, were recorded by Mr. Smithson of his own free will. The voice matches all known recordings, and psychologists of note have made it clear to us that it is almost impossible for the tapes to be the product of coercion. With its compelling need to keep moving, to encompass a lifetime in what Mr. Smithson may very well have believed to be his last hours, such a voice could not have been reading a prepared text.

We, therefore, reject the idea, originally suggested by his wife, perhaps his widow, Mrs. Alice Smithson (née: de Wonderland), that these tapes are the dictation of one or another Central American terrorist group, working here or back home, looking to discredit Wesley's work. In addition to the psychological assessment, it is hard to believe that any of the right wing death squads would have had the sense of humour; while the left-wing guerrillas, though at times demonstrating a distinct surrealist, or magic realist, poetic bent, are unlikely to have benefited from the results. This does not, of course, eliminate the possibility that either type of group may have sent the tapes. The stranger elements of the recording, which we take for humour, could conceivably represent only the spontaneous decay of Wesley's thought processes under the difficult conditions in which he may have spent his captivity. Such a conclusion would, however, make it most difficult to believe that Wesley Smithson is still alive.

It does, nonetheless, seem likely to us that the tapes represent a more sudden yielding to the isolation and stresses of his chosen profession. This is the thesis of his long time friend and close associate, photographer Rosalyn "the Red" Queen. She firmly believes that the tapes were recorded in his hotel room with his last remaining tapes within hours of being rescued from a ferris wheel where the pair had been stranded in the topmost car for six hours. The mechanism had broken down in what, in those parts of the world, is deemed a mild earthquake.

It should be noted that it is Ms. Queen's thesis on Wesley's sudden catastrophic collapse that many of Wesley Smithson's long time colleagues and friends find hardest to deal with. Although all are aware that Wesley had been encountering considerable professional and personal difficulties, of the kind often referred to as a crisis of conscience, prior to his last departure for Central America, none are willing to look at the toll these took on him, any more than they were ready to do more than drink with him when he needed them. We believe it is these so-called friends, in fact, who are behind Mrs. Smithson's recent change of heart as to the authenticity of the tapes. Her accusation that this paper has been the victim of an elaborate hoax, perhaps instigated, if not invented, by Ms. Queen, seems to stem from their mean-spirited gossiping.

At a public event shortly after Wesley's disappearance, Mrs. Smithson was overheard begging Ms. Queen to reconsider her position on the publication of the tapes.

"Think of the children," she said. "Don't you think they are better off as the offspring of an obscure journalist, than as the offspring of a cult figure, a well-known and admired *nut*?"

Manley Hardnews, Wesley's long time drinking buddy, who at that moment held Mrs. Smithson's elbow, was then heard to mutter under his breath, "You have nothing to worry about, Alice. Whatever the general public thinks, there isn't a newsman in the world who will think Wesley capable, under even the most extreme circumstances, of this sort of stream of consciousness aberration. Lazy, pretentious, emotional crap. That's what Wes would have said about this stuff. He would have cut his own balls off before he did this."

Then, looking at Rosalyn Queen, he continued, "They'll all know this horses—t to be the product of a troubled mind all right. But not Wesley's. He hated tape recorders. Even for interviews. Thought they were the worst thing to ever happen to journalism. Before word processors. This stuff comes out of the troubled— or should I say empty— mind of a jealous and hysterical broad."

We must here note that we give no more credence to these drunken accusations than we do to the more literal minded conclusions of that extreme group of Wesley's fans who may yet turn Wesley Smithson, the most thoughtful, if not sober, of journalists, into just that cult figure whose development Mrs. Smithson so fears. Taking up where the Kennedy assassination theory connoisseurs and UFO landing cover-up aficionados have left off, they have become the newest generation of conspiracy buffs. Due to certain mysterious references present in those tapes already leaked to them, they have undertaken the almost daily harassment of Ms. Queen.

These fans are under the impression that "the Red" knows the true whereabouts of Mr. Smithson, and that she can lead them to him before it is too late. They firmly believe that Wesley is being held captive in a sanitarium somewhere, not by guerillas, but by the CIA. They are sure he has been used, in yet another of the Agency's attempts to control the media, for some kind of bizarre journalistic mind control experiment whose results must be made public to the world. We can only hope that it was neither Mrs. Smithson nor Mr. Hardnews who leaked the tapes to this group of fruitcakes out of a purely vengeful desire to make Ms. Queen's life more difficult.

Despite these accusations, drunken and otherwise, from various quarters, and the more serious threat of a suit, we at this paper still maintain our belief that these tapes are the last known work of Wesley Smithson. And perhaps his best. We can only hope that you, as readers, can see them for what they are. Neither a hoax, nor a news story, nor a specially encoded secret message to those few who might be able to decipher it; but a brave man's final brief victory over his own terrible destiny. When all his interviews and event specific articles are forgotten, these tapes will stand as a monument to Wesley Smithson's profession and to his professionalism. In fear or in anguish, in pain or in doubt, at the edge of the big breakthrough or the total breakdown, Wesley Smithson stood firm to the last, his fingers on play/record.

In transcribing the tapes, we have tried to be as true to the voice on them as we could. We have changed nothing, confident that, with the opportunity for further analysis, meaning will one day be found in even what today seems most aberrant. The title and system of numeration are also Wesley Smithson's own.

(I)

The first one appeared last March. Directly after my return from Central America. At that time they said it was harmless. But then they always say it's harmless. Or that it will go away. Even with the news I write; they tell me that it will go away. Never accumulate: just go away until I do not know what makes me believe them. Or wish to, telling myself it will go away, go away never got away; we never say the stories get away even if they do, without corroborating evidence or a third source for difficulties already too dreadful to print, already too emotion filled for the objectivity that's a matter of pride, so that you keep it there, that terrible unconfirmed knowledge, on the epidermal layer where it can be sloughed off with the dead slabs of cells, it's perfectly harmless, shrugging or laughing and throwing your clothes into a corner where the chambermaid will pick them up for the laundry

to hand pound on cold stone washboards to leave the fibres thinner than they were before, but purer too I always feel, even the stink of death of fire of gunpowder of burning flesh or the slow rising perfume of bodies left to rot and be eaten in the sun, the contact smiling over them or looking away with his kerchief over his nose, and someone else leaning in the camera while I think how to phrase it, how to phrase it

eyes focused in the middle distance so that it will be equally palatable as the eggs with brown toast and strawberry jam eaten in a kitchen with flowered or cheerfully old fashioned copper utensil printed wallpaper; CLIFFSIDE GRAVESITE DISCOVERED, writes itself while the body's sweat grows so rancid that even the shower won't do and I decide to excise it or exorcise it, precision isn't always the answer

the way it was when they excised that one small spot, not it will go away but not to worry it will be all right, it's harmless they said, only they added probably, and snipped right around it, around that small black spot, an exact cut like a typewriter key hitting new bond, so precise, a carbon ribbon, no blurring at the edges, no uncertainty, this and only this is here, as they showed it to me and put it nicely, a piece of letraset now politely lifted from its plastic by the twinkling blade of an x-acto knife the doctor winking at me, onto its place on a slide, don't worry about it, nothing to worry about, you're in good hands; just what the whores would say

with the same bright smile and me laughing, oh yes, harmless completely harmless knife cutting flesh the keys cutting through carbon dust to hit the page black clean and easy and no scars and a beer or a highball glass lifting, an equally easy laughing, a well it's over another hard day over, and the others' smiles, hard days sure and well not to worry it will all be finished soon and we'll be somewhere else and more drinks all around whether they did anything that day or not, basking all of us

shirts from the laundry hanging in the sun or lizards on rocks, except even the lizards here don't bask they scurry, there are so many things here that scurry, in and out and around, the language and the people, experts in avoidance making us learn it too, except that we get to stop when we want, or mostly when we want, to bask or to squirm like the people on the dance floor: lizards wiggling out of their skins. And some as languid as the whores leaning on the bar stools just waiting. So that I laughed and leaned too. And only later wished I could have squirmed out of mine. When I had to admit how deeply my skin was attached to me as I said:

— Sure thing Doc, I'll be looking forward to hearing from you.

(1,2)

And I don't think I ever would have noticed it at all, that definite but indecipherable sign on my skin telling me that things don't always go away, never completely disappear, that they can leave stains or even cause lesions. If it hadn't been for taking overly long one day on the shitter

reading my wife's newest issue of *Chatelaine* there due to her one indulged impulse toward disorder, that never putting the magazines back in the little polished oak rack in the corner of the can to the left of the toilet but always leaving them spread, two or three, never more, on the hand laid Mexican tile, the plain clear glazed unpatterned stuff, the ones with the birds and flowers, each one different, are around the sink and the whirlpool, always interesting to contemplate

with lines you can follow around with your eyes and use to relax when it's a really big one, your eyes coming to rest on one spot, what my wife learned to do for the hardest part of labour, to concentrate and to push like when the haemorrhoids start to hurt, oh God now

to get it over with, a pain and pleasure at once that I've suffered from so long I can't remember a time without it, better and worse by moments in all that bouncing in jeeps and holding it in or going in places that don't bear mentioning any more than the sudden sharp pain that reminds you of never reported in detail things up the ass that you don't want to think about; images that creep into consciousness to make it impossible that particular day to just go on the visuals

on watching that white petal in the corner turn into a bird to eat a green insect that was a leaf that stretches its wing because the mind demands a linguistic distraction to fill it up until the unwanted horror can be pushed back out together with the huge turd, oh God, yes, so that I picked the magazine up

that little entrance into my wife's world so calm and smooth and on the surface even when overstuffed or rich like the food like page after page of ads for cake and ice cream and the newest frozen way to pretend you've cooked a meal, an abstract pleasantness like the airiness of the house, the solar panels and the sky lights and the bougainvillaea under them a tasteful reminder of the tropics my wife wouldn't tolerate a passion vine what will it do? she had said

all those tendrils they could find their way into anything, and besides the flowers were dull; which is true enough except up close where you can notice the strange hard inevitability of them decipher their coded reminiscence of Christ's Passion, something so perfectly Central American just like I told her

the missionaries finding them and sighing over their symbolism, their simple three nails five wounds and crown of thorns, pistils stamen and petals redolent and full, peaceful against the sun while the *conquistadors* were making the natives live their own far too realistic passion play, wounds alone by the million and more dramatic ways of execution than any three nails could ever accomplish: the very symbol of everything I wanted to get away from as she had not hesitated to point out snuggling up to win her way with the unquestionably lovely colour-coordinated bougainvillaea, her solid pink tongue sucking me into her mouth like the sticky hibiscus pistil, adding that she would take me away from all that out of breath with her hands in my robe, for sure she said, only to ask afterwards if that's what the girls said, you know, the girls down there, after they took me

while I laughed and ran my fingers down the white white skin of her belly and shrugged just the way I knew she wanted me to pardoning her her one small tropical exuberance, her inquisitive wish to be a flowering plant of multi-coloured blooms, do they do it this way or that? the sultry pale night blossom

as well as the daytime self as bright and transparent as the bougainvillaea suspended in the light, as sweet as all the cakes and candies and ice cream, as correct as the polishes and detergents and air fresheners and pictures of children playing

the occasional article to let her know what women today wanted, or needed or were thinking, how she could take care of her man, gourmet cooking and sexual competence, understanding his problems and the children's, or of herself if it came to that, in the world out there with a lawyer answering your questions on divorce and widowhood, what happens to the bank accounts the insurance policies

things I expect she thinks about though I never did strangely enough, not even with the startlingly beautiful young Latin society girl or revolutionary standing beside me, always I was too intensely loyal to that bright clear spot that was the well groomed life of her in the clean sheeted width of our bed, nor did the bullets whizzing by, being pulled over by the police, convince me death was real like the spot on my leg as I read that article that told me why she'd given up tanning

"Skin Cancer: a new danger under the tropical sun" that made me ask her what she thought it was, that strange spot new from the last trip, my finger pressing it until she looked up to focus on my leg, at least it wasn't my penis I fingered, at least it wasn't herpes I'd caught down there, and I hadn't said anything about AIDS, which made her smile

and pat the couch so that I would sit beside her, I was safe here, she said nuzzling me again, there's nothing to worry about here, and she touched me the way she did her porcelain vases, even with her lips, a prize possession once more safe in her house, and she patted my hand before going back to her magazine where there is always an answer to your question, always a remedy:

— See the doctor she'd said. Doubtless it's harmless.

(1,2,3)

And I had believed them. When they removed the first one I believed them. And later when the others started to show up I still believed them. Put my mind in order and recited her words again and made another doctor's appointment and believed them. The voices so sweet the words so imprecise that you cannot help but wish to drink them down, to rub yourself all over in baby oil and being convinced it can't happen here or to you because there are comforts in knowing that most writers most media men, no matter what anyone says, no matter what novels or movies use to amuse or astound the general public, live to a ripe old age or at worst an overripe middle one

and for those that don't it seems much more their own fault than not; and more than the walking into unnecessary danger it's the violent disorientation, the heat so strong or the evening chill, the sitting in a hotel room with bottle after bottle of cheap rum spitting it out brown at brown at the two and a half inch cockroaches that if you hit in the right season fly

or going to the market where even if you speak the language it's impenetrable; too many people who won't get out of the way of the car so that you get out and walk and the accents shouting out across the few empty spaces make the words incomprehensible with the laughter that always seems to come from behind as you walk by making you forget where you left the car while the big women cook and look you over commenting one to the other she didn't say that was iguana's tail soup did she? you want to ask again only you don't want to blow it to hear her laugh, derisive again so you just buy more rum and find your way back to the hotel room on foot and close the curtains and put on the air conditioning so that all you can hear is the hum and imagine yourself at home or maybe there's only a ceiling fan around and around again, whup whup whup whup hummmmm

you try to imagine it a carousel gentle like the light of the one twenty-five watt bulb, full of music and animals, tigers and lions maybe and oxen pulling carts and ponies, brightly harnessed ponies only all you ever get for an image is *Apocalypse Now* and the helicopters, the image of the fan and then the helicopters

dropping napalm, in the apocalypse that is still now because they still do that, always do that everywhere do that in your mind do that, or white phosphorus, accompanied by the children screaming from their burns or the blasts of bombs, tiny little pieces of metal embedded so much deeper in the flesh than moles while you want laughter and ice cream and try to keep it like home even if you never can keep it just the fan the friendly fan as you watch the mahogany go round and round

each of the four blades separately crafted, hand polished wood going by one after the other, casting their shadows on the ceiling or on you (whup whup whup whup) one two three four or four three two one or one three four two, it doesn't matter except that after a while you can tell them apart like the cars on the ferris wheel or the figures on the carousel the pony and the ox and the tiger and the lion, or the tiger and the ox and the lion and the pony, it doesn't matter at all which comes first or last or in the middle, napalm in Asia fragmentation bombs in Africa nerve gas in the Middle East white phosphorus in Latin America not at all, not ever

for the two or four rotor blades of the helicopter (whup whup whup whup) it matters only if it comes at all whether or not there is a place to hide if it does or that yours isn't the still living body about to be dropped out while the rest makes no difference; that car number four painted blue and re-painted in green is prettier than car number one painted in red over and over with the complementary coloured numbers right there on each side is just a slight distinction in decoration

the whole world made up of only slight differences in decoration a choice of bougainvillaea or passion flower purple until you convince yourself that even the letters of the alphabet by which you live are the same (whup whup whup whup) what what what what does it matter if it's A B C D or D C B A or Z X Y W or S H I T it's all the same anyway, just painted or printed or carved on the surface on the very top layer of metal or wood pulp or skin so that you distract yourself again thinking of the kids' faces, the faces of wood animals on a merry go round, the legs sticking out of the numbered cars of the ferris wheel

to make you weep maudlin tears for poverty or violence or just your own mediocrity because you're not the one who has the story that will bring it all down; which makes you take a magazine photo from the many stored in the photo morgue of your mind, not one your friend took in terrible conditions the day before but a cheerful tropical tour magazine picture you can slip into maybe of the things you will take home for gifts this time for the kids or the spacious new house maybe you'll even take the mahogany fan (whup whup whup whup) for your bed or living room because they're so good for air circulation if you smoke or your heating is uneven, especially in the winter believe it or not, as long as the hand crafted wood blades don't crack from the dryness, which makes it all truly much worse if the fan is broken because then there is no relief at all

from the edge of chaos not even four four time (whup whup whup whup) but just the voices that travel so far on the tropical air and maybe a radio here or there jagged and one dimensional, loud North American rock music which helps orient you a minute or it's *cumbia* or *mambo* and you imagine them dancing, you try to keep them dancing

in your mind around and around they go like the fan or the carousel, your own mental whup whup whup whup and far away like your own stupid thoughts of the natives being restless, they're so quiet most of the time when they're up to something, hunkered down maybe over the speaker of a small transistor like that one that was so expensive that you saw hanging in the market, in the shape of a ladybug, the kind you might buy for your ten-year-old daughter perhaps the only one they could afford and buying it for that, just to listen, sheltering it with their bodies, an infinitely precious creature or a prayer for listening to the guerrillas' clandestine radio

which makes you toss and turn for a while and try to adjust the sound or the silence to that back home sense which maybe doesn't work even if the air conditioner does, maybe you brought the trouble with you and see only the fights with the wife with the mistress with the kids when you close your eyes, one of them threw you out, you threw one of them out, maybe both to make you get up and stagger out to the market again to find one of the whores and bring her back

but all she does is walk around the room picking up your things and putting them down, what estrange theengs you have meester because what can you expect when you can't even get it up, what an estrange man you are meester? for sure she's seen it all before, all of it

while even the need for the comfort of someone else is drowned in that bottle which means that's all you remember her doing when you wake again, just her moving like a tracking shot in a 'B' movie with the buzzing no longer the air conditioning but just your head and so loud that when you venture out again you can't find the place where you could get rye whiskey to get off this rot gut rum, good Canadian rye whiskey at the American shop it was called except it doesn't matter

these days you don't have to show the passport if you have the greenbacks which means you don't even have to find an American to go with you, it's just that you can't remember the location and you don't want to ask and the sun hurts your head and twists your vision until you stagger even though you're just hung over which makes you want even less to go back to the place where the other journalists hang out, there's that French guy who's going to laugh at you again seeing you like this, the way he always winks and grins at you when you come in

sure you haven't got the story, not the good story, the one that's going to blow this place wide open the one everyone is always looking for; which means you head back to the market and duck into a banana leaf covered stall and the woman grins at you, you again meester and her smile hurts your head but the armadillo soup tastes good and you don't remember that you have ever been there

but you smile back anyway which maybe leads to her picking you up or maybe you just pick up the rum and you go back to your room and maybe you start living with her and collecting rare bugs in boxes or stringing scorpions on chains and maybe they say you've gone native or they just say crazy and circle their ears with their forefingers because everybody knows even you no matter how bad off you are by then that you can go as native as you want but you still can't go the distance

so it's just falling further and further into chaos until by the time you get back to your hotel room it's already with the violent dysentery complement to the violent disorientation or to just the violence which is maybe what sent you into that hole to start with, or maybe you've stayed there all along and when they come for you it's by the smell

and the word of mouth at the bars, people asking if you've left and nobody knows; and maybe it's already rot or maybe just your own shit or vomit that stinks but when they haul you out it's unconscious or dead and after that it's game over except for the arrangements. Which I'm sure my wife for one has imagined day after day,

at least once a week playing the scene again and again to be sure she will have it down, she will know how to behave, in tranquilizers and tasteful black with a few tears and the drink taken with a shaking hand, just enough to wet the throat but not

enough for loss of control with the others standing around as the American photographer comes up to squeeze her arm and says:

— And he was so good. The best. Too bad he never got the recognition, the big break, he deserved.

(1,2,3,4)

So that I'm always careful to keep my distance, my sense of place. My sense of who they are and who I am and never go with a woman who isn't a real professional of some sort, men or cameras or stories, not that I think it's bad, or wrong

the natives I mean, just that problem of identifying with them, of having to make sure it's never quite a total identification, that you know the difference, like with fluffy white bread and flat yellow tortilla: it's all ground grain flour of some sort but it doesn't taste the same or do the same to your insides. Because it's coming to not know the difference that kills you in this business, that not keeping your perspective on things that pushes you over that very fine line. Without the necessary cool edge to the voice you lose your objective understanding of the full range of human degradation and cruelty and even its counterpoint in the beauty of it all, which makes it easy to get all tangled

to become part and not an observer which you'll never know how to handle any more than most of them do, being part of that, because they die of violent disorientation in corners too for years and years before any of us see them before the cameras doing fashion fun in the sun start to pick them up, don't kid yourself

it may take a short time to learn to make a molotov cocktail but it's a long time before they lock on target and start doing it together and my agent calls me to go do an in-depth article on the latest hot spot as if the front burner just got turned on last night a contagious excitement in that it's Central America again this time Wes which builds up in me too as he tells me that at least I know something about it, have a long history there which makes it better than starting over again in South Africa I suppose, with all my memories of the young in the streets to carry me through the high cumulus build-up on the flight

but then no matter where you go it's mostly the young, maybe some of the old have been in it for years but mostly they're the ones who are still drinking themselves to death in their shacks where we don't see them and I refuse to imagine them, places where they've never heard of air conditioning or used fans and the breeze and the voices come in through the chinks in the wood slats or maybe it's just corrugated cardboard from those big crates

like the ones from the new dishwasher and refrigerator my wife purchased last summer when I was away, the crates the kids used to make a fort, so that the voices, the laughter sweet talk or screams are never absent, there's nothing to cover them, not even the few sun faded magazine pictures of a faraway life if not place pinned to the cardboard walls will do, which means it hurts them too, unbearably sometimes

that chaotic noise; except the silence hurts more, the army or the National Guard or the death squads looking for the kids again until they hit the cockroach when they spit their *aguardiente* transparent at brown, it's all they can do to pretend to shit on the brown uniform of the guard, what they never dared do when they still had the coordination, so that I never think of that you can't want to be part of that no matter how romantic its manifestations which no one is above fantasizing especially at 45,000 feet and banking above it all, what a life it could be, trekking deep in the green green repeat green jungle or underground in the sordid city, right in the middle of it, knowing how it feels

at least it helps me to relax to move those guerrilla dolls around when I'm on the plane or in any moving vehicle on my way back or forth, contained in a contraption whose estimated place of arrival I can visualize though mostly myself I fantasize the story, that this time or next time depending on my destination it will be the big story

the one that will break a country, a whole society, an entire way of life wide open, that will change the course of history like being the one to take the picture when Somoza's National Guard shot that American, or the one to get the hard evidence the unimpeachable sources that know beyond the shadow of a doubt who gave the order

for the death of an Archbishop, any number of possibilities as long as someone, someone with credibility is forced to say the unsayable; which is easily dangerous enough though maybe too real without adding some little superficial underground adventure to stop you filling up completely with anxiety, or knowledge

of what it is you're walking into, horror or danger disguised in beautiful hotels like the doctor's smile so that I'm not above drinking myself through an acute attack either with elegant motions that accept the surface glow as the only reality or just sitting with my hands fastened hard to the armrests mind empty of all images bargaining with God as the airplane bottoms out of a downdraft trying to land in the Valley of Mexico. Only I do try to restrict it

like I do thinking about the spots on my skin even if I am about to stop the car and park it illegally in the doctor's parking lot or the plane to land, still it isn't good to use that one too often, or to need the crutch of your discrete North American reality too badly. Whether or not you take Him particularly seriously it's just too heavy to have to sit and mumble, your lips moving slowly, that prayer of:

— Please God please. Just this time please: let me see my wife and children again.

(4,1,3,2)

Because after that it's not just magazine pictures in the mind. But the wallet size photos that start coming out in the middle of the night as you start touching the wood of the shutters, or the walls, the fan always too high to reach and besides it's moving. Though maybe the ritual does help ward away the worst demons if you're careful not to overuse it, all that loyalty and the smiles and the paper smooth image of the house. Even going down to the Hilton to buy one, any magazine though the concrete connection makes ladies' better, the need to physically touch the wood pulp icon of the ice cream or the gourmet popcorn to be reminded where you're really from, what side you're on

at least of the camera or typewriter; so that it's with the aching desire for sure knowledge that you can go home again that you will always be able to go home that you sit down in that little park to watch the ferris wheel go up up up and around

into the dense and powdery passion flower pale purple twilight its coarse metal frame held to the ground by children's laughter, the children coming around to ask for hey meester so many *soles* or *pesos* or *quetzales* or *colones* or *cordobas* to go up up up and around that you give them or entrust to the oldest to share fairly with the younger brothers and sisters not so much out of pity for their old clothes, the slight worn rips that make them just a slightly denser twilight or paler dawn or even for their plastic shoes with the little holes or their inches thick shoe leather brown calluses where the hook-worm can crawl in; but out of love, a single gesture of love a little for them but mostly a kiss to the sky for the winds to carry to your own children in a gesture finally more of luck, a metaphysical crossing of fingers, a formula that if you follow surely surely there is no question but home home again to sit under the one bright bougainvillaea

strung along the skylight while you examine maybe dozens of other flat but dramatic magazine pictures that the woman sitting next to you on the ferris wheel took whose captions you will write so that you smile a bright smile that glows like the orange metal bars against the sky and let out a laugh that carries with the darkening movement of the leaves, the birds coming to rest black against the dense scent of jasmine

and you feel content maybe even happy your calm restored, a perfectly oriented evening here and there at once that just this one time makes you take your companion up on her invitation to go up up up and around in that ferris wheel yourself just as soon as you finish the orange yellow mango ice cream, just this once c'mon just this once

a camera-draped American photographer and sure why not it must be safe enough the little rust on the bright painted metal is nothing they must care about the kids, a care that's always manifest in the concrete of objects to the best of their ability or availability of materials

which makes me look carefully at the merry-go-round later the round and around of its wood carvings with so much passionate earth in them, the layers of paint the *carnaval* mask stiffness of the poses the carefully carved horns of the staid and solid oxen, the hieratic majesty of the lions with their stiff manes, the spirited self-parody of the ponies mouths open in surprise, the carnivorous ferocity of the tigers their heads veering off watchful toward inside and out

things twenty thirty forty fifty or more years old with all the power of primitive and loving conception, the transition from the frontal to the three dimensional so notable so often in that kind of thing according to my companion who watches me run my hands over them as she tells me I should see her collection of Mexican dance masks

especially the ones where the hyenas just begin to turn their heads that are on her wall in Washington, except that it was more the layering, that they had been painted so many times that got to me, that made me love them, all those strange marks a whole history's marks on their silent skin; only maybe it wasn't the art at all

whether I loved it or not that made me do it, but just impressing her after the ferris wheel that made me buy the tigers and the lions and the oxen and the ponies, the whole merry-go-round except the plank floor and metal frame, all the carving, even the stuff in the centre octagon with the mirrors

all of it shipped home for no more than a couple thousand all together because I got them in duty free as art pieces so that the guy who owned them got it all, I'm kind of sorry it wasn't the people who made them, but even him, he just stood there with his mouth hanging open like one of his own carvings disbelieving he would ever see the money disbelieving it I think even when the truck arrived as I disbelieved the plane carrying them would ever arrive and will not believe that I will ever see my mental image of my kids riding them under the bougainvillaea or out in the garden shouting with tropical voices because even that image cannot come true until I find time to unpack the tiger and the ox and the pony and the lion until I take a moment to stop thinking of my work to consciously put to the back of my mind again the new red spots on my skin or the ferris wheel that goes round and round up over and down in my mind

as I rise toward the doctor's office in that elevator with its walls the same colour as the twilight sky; a casual scratchy texture as uncomfortable under my hand with the elevator rising as the old plywood, splintered and repainted the colours bleeding through from layer to layer, was under my butt as the ferris wheel started skyward over the city and we looked out toward tall buildings and over cardboard slums where the well-to-do are those with papaya trees and the comfortable those who build their fences with the uselessness of gladiolus the same orange scented with deep blue as the fast fading edge of the sky

and the breeze blue against us in that brilliant timeless moment before something happens: a pause like an intake of breath or a sneeze, for right before the penetrating tremor of a quake, something you could never understand if you haven't been in one, or at least heard an avalanche the moment of silence when you feel it before the groan announces its presence

with your balance destroyed like in the hours after walking out of the plane, the same lack of trust in the placement of the ground after that terrible possibility of rising and falling of not quite being where you are in a tin can in the sky and only the droning motors keeping you up, like knowing your life will only last as long as you can keep putting energy into it

so that you become afraid of letting go, of armrest or alertness, until you're identified with each creak in the metal, each wobble of the wings, and the frame of the wheel that shimmies just ever so slightly out of alignment and a groan from below as you see exactly where the structure wants to pull apart while the children on the ride scream still with the edge of delight because you know the groan would have to be much louder before they got really scared

at least that's what you tell yourself as you cross your fingers, they're not scared they must know as you wait for that one louder noise that will collapse so many houses as it has before, here and so many theres, to create whole areas where only the hard tropical grasses or the wild passion vine grows or hanging laundry blooms bright against cardboard temporary room partitions placed on concrete floors without walls

slum dwellings laid over luxury apartments something for future archaeologists to contemplate, the counter-evolution of physical culture in underdeveloped or maybe it's counterdeveloped, areas, the reinforcing rods hanging out like bones over each floor of those high rise shantytowns the old bones buried far below

other times other places other quakes, and that day just a small memento of the rising stink of cities where substandard building practices have accomplished a death total in an hour that usually takes the death squads at least a year, six months during really bad times

with the bodies left to rot in the business as usual of laziness or greed terror and intimidation, in the end it's all the same, a kind of fatal lack of attention to the future, death in active or passive voice and my mind starts to write headlines again: a human interest story a local tropical colourful story in another series of words marching in formation across a page accompanied by pictures except that even so perfect an antacid the bromide so well developed over the years can't stop my stomach from turning over

at the very top of the arc; and I do not so much remember as feel again the first time I ever smelled that death smell, weeks of it those Somoza days after the Managua quake looking at the Bank of America the only building left standing while up up but not around I think that my number has come up

that this time I deserve the real thing. When the man below stops the motor to wait it out and I panic. Panic and say it all to myself again very quickly and under my breath

with absolute determination looking away into the trees please God please just this once, just this once with my fingers crossed as my knuckles turn white as I grab on hard to the wooden bar of the seat the steel rod of the frame as my companion puts her well manicured short nailed photographer's hand on my knee, still so polite, to say:

— Don't worry, it happens all the time in these countries. But you must know that.

(3,4,1,2)

And I looked away and held on tighter and hissed out a yes. Because she had said that twice that day. It happens all the time in these countries. Earthquakes and torture and disappearances: a day spent listening to testimony translated by a nun who knew the local lingo all too well

going from person to person of those in her parish who knew or who had experienced such things. And my companion holding more onto herself than to me: it happens all the time in these countries and me no reaction at all except that delayed reaction high up in the sky and not to action so much as to inaction

to helplessness to not being able to do anything to climb down or off just suspended in the middle of the thick hot air the tenuous colour of a story whose inexorable movement toward its end you cannot stop so that you wonder if you can stop or change anything; only you can't quite shrug so you hold on tighter and because you don't want to shake or to sob

you just say again that please God please let me go back, just this once let it happen the way my mind said it would when I left just a slight inconvenience a slight shake in the earth a fold in time an aside in the one story you have lived over and over that brings down absolutely nothing

not a society not a way of life not even the finally fragile metal frame of a ferris wheel but yes you to earth coming true again and again the personal myth of the permanent resolution, the plane ride and down at the airport walking along the plastic partitioned corridors the texture like this elevator only you know what is at the end of the corridor there is no question or reason to panic like I do now to think how it's no longer a long tunnel but a closed off square

or open, but anyway a small box in the middle of the air from which there is no decisional escape as I wonder if yes, this time my loan's been called in because maybe I've said it just once too often my favourite please, God, please just once more home home again

the kids coming out to greet me, to throw their little arms around me still in the same t-shirts or bright coloured ponchos that the last trip bought and smelling of bubble gum as the wife hangs back just a little the smile always just a little frightened animal at first hiding its doubt in the corner of her lips where the lipstick smears and then bright like the magazines and as perfectly rigid, this is the right scene isn't it? this is the husband returning? and then bigger and brighter till it's

just herself now, no staging no questions, bright as mountain sun or when we first got to know each other, and then she can't wait a second more, and her feet carry her to me too, her arms around the kids and around me, and please God just once more and then you can have me any time you want me as long as it's in my bed looking out the window at the weeping birches, black and white with the snow or the rich summer browns and greens

anything but get me off this wheel out of this place; so that it's hard to believe this is happening to even keep going now to not break down and scream to keep my hand relaxed and gentle against those lumps of silk

as I acknowledge the elevator will not stop in the middle of up up and over but only at the right floor that I must follow a predetermined trajectory with only one possible termination no matter how long the corridors no matter how the prisoner attempted to slow his step as he walked or crawled or was carried to that final door you too know is there

and watched it opening; slow like the stories that inevitably dead end, the teller's voice halting for the change in point of view, where she must cease to be participant to become observer too, cool or sobbing because she knows that her imagination can only encompass the door gone through, never the secret bloody insides of helicopters

or the feelings of the cut open still living bodies about to be thrown from them, any more than I could take in, than I could digest or metabolize or think through or make myself look at that sense of ending in the blood red spots on my body

to comprehend what there was just around the corner just outside the door as I tried to forget that this time I was any more than the most peripheral of the cast of characters, just the hearer, maybe just the witness, the one who at most saw someone taken away but that's all, it's only them

it's only my skin it's not me, it's only on the surface it's far away it won't come any closer this is someone else's experience my bough never breaks the swinging cradle of my ferris wheel car never falls everything is always all right is always someone else. Said in mental march rhythm down the hall as I organized my slowly shifting thoughts like story notes as I stepped forward one foot in front of the other until I was ready to face the Doctor to utter my usual silly, racquet ball partner jovial:

— What's up, Doc?

(2,3,4,1)

Having determined to think of the merry-go-round and how I would reward myself by finally unpacking it. For sure, today, as soon as I got home, even if my wife did still object that they wouldn't go, they'd be too large, they'd make a mess, maybe they had termites. Because I knew she would love them in the end, especially the tigers

but the ponies too, and the kids would take so easily to the lions and the oxen, just a little touch of old art under the bougainvillaea, such things were so in this year, even she said that, a touch of complexity to go with the high tech metal and they would be so genuine so authentic

absolutely no one else would have anything like them just there in the perfect spot where some nutty friend or another could be counted on to ride them margarita in hand but maybe that was what she was afraid of or that they would drive me

cuba libre in hand to tell stories, baffling and bloody the stories she never wants to hear, the ones without 'the moral of this story is' tacked on at the end that make her say shsh shsh take your mind off it just the way the doctor does

spinning around on his soft vinyl covered stool his hand on some form of needle so that I think that I will tell all those guests who will surely drop by how generous I was to buy the carousel, how happy the man was to have that money, how he'd never seen so much together in his life how I gave it to him even though I knew he overcharged me, enough anyway for that little travelling amusement park to put together another merry-go-round because they could still get someone to do the carvings cheap, those kind of craftsmen, and they're good craftsmen, are still a dime a dozen down there, maybe Walt Disney characters this time, I had seen those upon occasion or dinosaurs from the Flintstones only with the same primitive intensity

of desire moving from two into three dimensions and then four around and around to the music, every two years or so another coat of paint and then around again, a very generous gesture that one I had made, no one has ever said I am not a generous man

I always pay the people who help me quite well after all I depend on them, you could tell how much it was to him by the way he counted it, and how he invited his friends over to see, I hope they didn't help him to drink it, I never did go back to see how he did with it, and you never know with those people you just do your best to make them dependable

and fairness and generosity help which is why I appreciate it in others, the doctor's generosity did help me to be in a cheerful frame of mind thinking so calmly of how well on balance I have behaved in my travels

envisioning those animals, the oxen and the ponies and the tigers and the lions that have come home with me to my living room as he takes his time to reassure me so carefully how perfectly harmless those spots are or that they come out as we get older and I laugh to myself a warm internal chuckle to hear him say they call them cherry angiomas cherry angiomas we call them he says, a small tumour full of blood but perfectly harmless a cheery name I think for things full of blood but then we try always to call blood by cheery names, even bloodbaths, give them perfect contained little explanations no danger of spreading explanations

always harmless he repeated, this kind never turns into cancer, the small lesions just stay on the surface each one sealed off right below or right in the epidermal layer I think he said, no danger of wandering off anywhere else of penetrating any deeper

that's nice is all I believe I answered but I remember thinking bleeding hearts always do, stay on the surface that is, in small compartments, the only possible danger each one growing as big as that first one he was poking right under my left nipple

a disgusting thing about a quarter inch around and puffy my bleeding heart above my heart and just like he said, it's hardly a danger for a man, for the wife maybe, but hardly for a man except maybe a very vain man, one who likes to show off his body

which could hardly have meant me, except to be joking about more than enough to show off, not that I don't get around, all over the world in fact, and my heart's fine but he looked at me strangely anyway, and the fact was

harmless or not they did bother me and I said it without thinking, lost in my thoughts of tigers and lions and oxen and ponies I invited him to take them off, especially the big one on my chest, yes off my chest, I wanted it off my chest and I laughed, off off, all of them off nobody needs tiny bleeding hearts all over his body even if they are always harmless always only skin deep still those memories of my fear wouldn't always be easy to deal with. Tiny blood full lesions where everybody could see if I ever wore a bathing suit, I might even start to cry in public, I didn't care what he thought at this point it just wouldn't do. So I shrugged and asked him what the procedure was.

— We burn them out, he said. With electricity, he added, while picking up a shapely pink plastic-handled instrument whose curved metal point he prepared to bring into contact with my flesh.

(2,1,3,4)

After which he told me he could freeze the big one. Which was fine by me. So numb already that I just said yeah. Yeah. The big one. Yeah. I can deal with the rest without anaesthesia but the big one yeah. Yeah yeah. Around in circles, yeah. A merry-go-round yeah yeah freezing the mind until the buzzing started

and the odour of burning flesh rose to my nostrils, of flesh that I could distinguish as mine in the small tugs to the neighbouring tissue, that tiny disturbance in the usual arrangement of the territory

like what the neighbours must feel when someone in the shantytown fails to come back, maybe burned too, and they shiver maybe or shake the way my arm did, wanting to ask the doctor for a drink but there was no way to forget the pride, desert the silent self-centred suffering in the hand grabbed on to the metal side of the bench hidden there below me where he couldn't see

while I felt a gasp rising in the throat which I couldn't turn into words, it was such an insubstantial pain to the psyche like it always was with all those stories I had ever heard, that pain that is always almost but never quite

my flesh, something that you can barely allow yourself to feel and never say even as my head turned automatically to look around the room which was suddenly as far away as the ground from the ferris wheel my stomach up up and almost over, frozen somewhere in the middle of a breath, and everything so small the tiny green table like a shanty far below, and my eyes measuring that space so small it was

not more my God than four paces long and two across, how much is that? I didn't know, three and a half metres by two maybe or eleven by six feet, the size of a small suburban bedroom and then its two tasteful tables and two chairs and the one spinning stool and all the equipment hanging on the walls

things with which to burn and things with which to cut and things with which to poke and prod and look into, all of them in pinks and greys, plastics of course, from the hard handle of the instrument he was burning me with, its coiled telephone style pink wires stretched behind it, to the soft grey vinyl of the table covering beneath the white paper under my sweating butt

my face sweating too so that the few gleams of metal of polished steel or aluminum, the stirrups I didn't need and that little tweezer he held in his other hand they winked at me brighter and brighter like sun through water the sickening lurch of heatstroke as I looked at the pointed hook of that instrument that burned me its bent end blackened from previous burns so that when he was finished I got up, the slight dizziness still in my head the weakness in my limbs

a flush in my cheeks that made me fan myself as I walked to the window to part one piece of hanging blind from another to widen the slit of natural light entering the room until it fell across the green carpet in a long triangle

where looking down over the city still green around the edges and the sun reflecting off the glass in the windows of the one tall building across from us I wanted to ask him if he knew that the Bank of America was the one tall building left standing when the earthquake hit Managua or why Ilopango airport was so many miles from San Salvador

not for the same reasons as Mirabel I wanted to tell him; it was the beautiful beaches that were supposed to attract the tourist trade, a perfect journalistic aside to show my concern for the world and lack of concern for what he was doing to my body, except I wasn't thinking of the terrible devastation so close to light and sand and brilliant luxury I was too close to the edge myself and just needed to keep repeating how

that brown below wasn't the brown of shantytown or rubble that the sun shone kindly there that the sun is kind on all those beaches and the Pacific coast of El Salvador one of the most beautiful in the world and this city too is lovely, the view's lovely I said, and the doctor's office so well appointed and much much larger than any room they might use for interrogation

or electric torture and surely the tables and machines are, if not so very different at least more prettily designed to disguise their function not brag of it for all that on that little one he rolls around you can always see if you look the meters

that calculate precisely how much current runs, measured in amps or volts I can never remember which measures current I know it's not watts, that's light bulbs; nor remember, however often I have been told by the experts

which levels of whichever cause extreme pain and which death or at least permanent damage, the statistics thrown out onto the page disappear from mind once written down, a drink and a forced disappearance like the burned-out mole from my skin, there won't even be a little scar he says nothing to show my bleeding heart was there, thinking that's why I turn away

and try to hang on to my glass or the metal edge of the seat or the window ledge without admitting that's what I'm doing but I can't stop thinking how surely those machines would not be plastic handled and coated and polite and there is a window here and a linoleum floor, it isn't concrete or covered in piss and shit with no antiseptic for the wounds or chemically arrived-at jasmine scented air-freshener to rapidly cover the smell while I feel the world give way under me

the ferris wheel finally starting down the weakness in my limbs as the sudden upward breeze penetrates my shirt to wake them into time and into relief as I finally escape the patterned repetition in the hand squeezing the metal bar, tighter looser tighter looser that says over and over, up up and over I'm not really here

I'm not really here nothing has really happened not to me not to me not to me because I hear it now penetrating for the first time to the medulla the hind brain the emotions so that I can understand

what he has been saying; what all his words add up to clear as the transparent waters of the Caribbean all the brilliant fish of opening future possibility swimming in different directions there below, harmless again he said harmless the relief a current now, not electric the Gulf Stream a spring tide in an estuary or the wind as I just let the ride go on and on, on and up and on and over and on and down and on and up again, again and again and again and again as we giggled like the children and clapped our hands and threw back our heads and I finger the curtain and I laugh with him as he laughs at me and I don't care

at all what he thinks not a bit about that knowing look I see reflected in the window as he thinks he's watching another case of cowardice overcoming vanity standing there like that with that pink wand still in his hand a rabbit toothed fairy godmother that has just given me my wish its cord stretched out while my eyes fix on the bus

blue and white and metallic gleam the size of a large cockroach in the vision that I wish I could spit at as I notice for the first time all the nausea produced saliva that has been sitting in my mouth

while I let it crawl away choking a little and swallowing hard as I await the final moment of over. Over and down and the car stopping and the man pulling back the bar as I tell him I've changed my mind that I'll keep the rest

while I touch a very small tumour an inch or so from the bandaid over the raw spot left by the one he has removed and I add with a wink, resigned ages ago to the contradiction that is so often there between what you know and what you say or write, between word and subvocalized thought:

— Every journalist needs a few small bleeding hearts.

(2,4,1,3)

Because who would ever admit in the spanking clean of his office to trying to feel in the so light and so professional touch of the moment that he cut, the edges. To trying to feel at least the outline

as of an embossed letter. A message for the hand not as definite as braille. There if you could just decipher its hollows; your eyes closed. Always closed even as you try to analyze the slight red to purple toothachy glow of the mistreated flesh the bright yellow sear of the burn that only begins that pain the tortured must feel

because of course I had thought it. Watching that pink handled instrument I had thought: is this what it's like to be tortured? just like I do sometimes when I hear it, all that testimony, and feel a contraction in my crotch a slight unnoticeable hardening the unadmittable evidence of that anxiety between pain and pleasure that is too close to that other anxiety that is definitely pleasure

still there after all these years when I get into the can; calling into mind the image of a movie star I will never have or a girl, a woman, a friend seen in the streets or at parties or whose warm thigh once bounced against mine minute by minute in a jeep

or whose casual acquaintance I make holding out the new cookie mix in the magazine on the floor or worst of all the ones that sometimes make me want to slap it down instead of rubbing it tenderly up and back the nauseous edge of building my rhythm to the flat flat images of the wet pussies of *Penthouse* or *Playboy* or some such other the pussies' flat words below

holding their hardened nipples to say I am nineteen and love adventure I dream of being a photojournalist or model of going to the real ho-ot spo-ots written like that while her finger massages the only hot spot she'll likely ever get to and I watch unable to let her go

oh those hot spo-ots in increasing fascination always one version or another of the same story, the way you feel after awhile about everything: it's always the same story and never the one to bring down a whole society an entire way of life, just enough for a few minutes and a few million dicks

to bring them up and over and down; our common occupation or preoccupation with the right houses and the right stereos and the right girls and the right stories all the right accoutrements what I tell my wife I buy those magazines for, all those stories that almost almost they're so good really so very goo-ood

exposing so much more than just the pussies only it's never quite enough to get more than a quick climax to get a clear picture because in the end those stories are still just part of the image the window dressing the *haute couture* of the pimp's bid to make himself respectable which doesn't mean I still wouldn't like to write for them

it wouldn't bother me so much to know that as usual especially when you run a high class string it's the girls and not the little extras that pay the rent; because it's all part of an understanding that doesn't help at all any more than closing the magazine does because I do love it sometimes like pulling off scabs or over-scratching mosquito bites until they bleed or the feel of the big shit coming out right there behind the stiff dick through the bleeding haemorrhoids as I think

I shouldn't I shouldn't oh and I tell the doctor that no I wouldn't please thank you after all no, and could never ever tell him or anyone else why as I turned my back on the temptation of the needle on that plastic possibility of just a little bit of that pain like flinging the magazine in self-inflicted fury across the floor while her image still stays in my mind and yes I imagine it

I cannot stop that part, what it must be like to be caught and held and tied smaller even than a cockroach a millipede a maggot in someone else's eyes your captors' or your captors' masters', taking up less space than that bus does in my sight from far above it and never so bright coloured

even with the temporary or permanent welts, never bright coloured like me in the same urban transport blue and white trimmed in the tasteful tree on the sidewalk green of my genuine fifties Hawaiian shirt, but just plain cockroach brown oh God

to be just cockroach brown and someone spitting rum on the raw the very hot and burning spots of your wounds and you so small and far away from help and pinned down the way I have never been pinned down, it's something we never even get close to we can always move or try; always at the very least crawl away like the bus moving, away even from that small pointed plastic instrument whose services are no longer needed laughing and repeating it's harmless it's harmless whether it's good or bad right or wrong it's harmless

to imagine what will never pin me down because even my words of telling the firm black on the white or yellow of the paper cannot pin me down, none of it can pin me down, it's all just another shell like the house that doesn't pin me down

not a cell or a limitation but the famous place to come home to always a place to come home to in spacious rooms and gardens and the perfectly mixed drink the historic definition of events the statistical limits

everything calm and pristine and reserved each hair or letter or throw pillow or bougainvillaea leaf in its place nothing stepping out of bounds because the letters have not yet migrated off the page I am free to come and go as I please as I can stay in this office if I want, yes, just a touch more current please

or go; listen to or make a tape of or turn my back on or walk away from all those testifying before me in their slowed Central American Spanish full of swear words and occasional eloquence and held down or blanked out or loudly expressed emotion patting them on the shoulder or the arm or even the cheek to say goodbye, letting the tears rise to my eyes sometimes the way they did to the eyes of my American friend that day she had to take the pictures

of those terrible welted scars they will always have to live with, getting as close as she could posing them for the best view almost like the models in one of those magazines, I remember one slack mouthed old lady with only her skirt left on a classic cheesecake picture arm above her head to let the camera capture, that's it, that's it, just a little more now, turn a little to me the arm a little higher now, not a perfect nubile outthrust right breast turned perfectly to dominate the frame but the one long scar

where the breast had been; and not removed by any careful mastectomy though still a clean cut from her husband's *machete* the one that had always hung on the stick wall of the hut, used first to decapitate him so that my friend did have problems then who knows

whether tears or the focus the way she assured me later when she said it happens all the time in these countries yawning as if nothing ever bothered her only her voice was too flat even for that earlier oh fuck this Wes

I brought the wrong lens as she insisted that we go and I packed the microphone away into its pocket and laughed to hear her swear again behind me a kind laugh I thought it was, though we never did go back, a bit of relief in it too for knowing that I wouldn't have to, what I imagine in the doctor's chuckle over by the window, human foibles and the knowledge that at least I was all right at least

some of the ones who come to him are all right, like my knowing those people are all right, a little damaged but all right, a chuckle for the ones who came with only certain small pieces lopped off out the other end of the sausage making machine, at least that one small it's over now carried some weight although you could never tell them not to worry still it had some meaning, that way we looked at each other as we passed under the wood linteled doorway of the old adobe house and touched hands to whisper at least it's over for them, they had escaped the event beyond imagining that neither my mind nor crotch will seek out where what approaches the body

is not a polite pink plastic-handled needle or even the torturer's cattle prod but a burning brand, a hot rod, an image that starts me into a harsher crueller chuckle into just one shake of the body to say

thank God those things never happen to never even come near people like me. Just a few harmless bleeding hearts for optional burning, so simple a complaint that I'm sure my relief shows all over

to influence his returning smile, the one in which his teeth no longer seem so very big as I say just what I said that day except that then it was in a different more awkward language that never quite responds to the efforts of my tongue. Shaking trembling hands patting scarred shoulders looking into faces whose eyes looked away as I said:

— Thank you very much for your time and trouble, but I gotta go now.

(3,2,4,1)

Only to get home still so numb over my heart that I numb myself still more on the high class rum I brought back from my last sojourn as I start to unpack the merry-go-round animals. And try to remain numb enough to get through yet another one. It was so good to feel reprieved, to feel that I was on Grace to feel that nothing could now happen to me

that I had even whistled in anticipation for days as I alternated unpacking the lions and the tigers and the oxen and the ponies with packing my shirts and my pants and my socks and my underwear, finishing each day with drinks under the bougainvillaea singing as I awaited what I knew was the inevitable phone call to confirm the new assignment

childishly excited to be able to say of course I'd go, I was free and clear and no encumbrances it had been a good time home all things considered and this time my wife and kids could meet me in Cozumel when I was through, my loan from God had not been called in, I was convinced He'd cancelled it for services rendered

all the horror I'd had to tolerate without any of it happening to me, an absorbent sponge; which made it so nice to think of getting some sun and the kids learning to SCUBA dive on their Christmas break

all of us watching the shadows of the sea urchins like purple poinsettias in the undersea twilight the phosphorescent tips of anemone tentacles like stars bright blue and yellow fish twisting in and out of complex calcite and coral the glimpse of rock lobster or shrimp and of course I would go

I felt so light with the weight of my largest little bleeding heart removed that I could still think all my lesions superficial and limited making it easy to write the right stories this time, some minor little quakes of stories that might scare the uninitiated or make the veteran hang on tighter but nothing to bring anything down

as we'd all sit around in the bars and I would think that none of it could possibly hurt me that none of it could ever be more than skin deep and so easily excised by that simple operation of saying just a few more times like for the beads of a rosary

how terrible it was; how simply awful, how you hoped they would get over it soon this penchant for violence no one could or should have to live like this it would be so good if they could just overcome their ignorance

such attractive people despite the poverty well nothing to be done for it but hope or pray for the best for someone somewhere coming to his senses and in the meantime well enjoy enjoy because there's nothing for that either but to pass the time as best you can beautiful women and lovely crafts and good service and this here's the life, eh Charlie, and it could be a very long one just hanging out while human nature insisted once more on making the worst of a bad situation

and I'll drink to that but only once or twice no one out of the whole press corps drinking himself to death in hotel room or bar or dying in a brawl over some two-bit whore, no one going off to open a brothel, no one at all balanced on the edge this time around, no violent disorientation of any sort, only enough of the exotic to make it beautiful and refreshing like the subtle difference between hibiscus and amaryllis so that I didn't panic at all, not even mildly not even once but concentrated

on the sun when it was out and the glowing wet flowers when it wasn't and savoured the flavour of my reprieve even on the buses or in the cars or the jeeps crowded or armed and going through the huge puddles of the end of rainy season so that even when I noticed the spots as I lay on the beach with my wife my head in her sun shaded lap my body still roasting slowly half buried in the sand, even when I saw those little marks with their funny dark centres and the old newsprint yellow to tan faded surrounds I didn't even remember

to pay attention; that woman's article had long skipped my mind which meant I just considered them a kind of combination of freckle and mosquito bite or bee sting with those precise centres like where those bugs stick whatever it is they stick in like a small bull's eye, even a metaphorical target in the middle didn't bother me or maybe I just found them amusing

the way my wife did freckle on freckle, I had so many of them she said touching one, there hadn't been room for any more, like crowding in third world cities, the thousands moving to them each week, these must be all the unemployed freckles in the world migrating onto my body which must seem a great mecca to them so much of it and well cared for she giggled affectionately poking my well oiled belly they now had to move in one on top of the other and we both laughed

affectionately and she sipped her piña colada and I watched the liquid rise translucent through its long plastic straw before I called the boy to bring me another *cuba* and wiggled my toes farther down into the sand to try to find the start of damp the start of cold as the ghost crabs went to ground for yards around me and I ran

my hand along my wife's white white thigh that never darkened with that number 22 PABA cream she kept rubbing in and pulled one tiny red pubic hair that stuck out from her shorts, a tiny blade of wife skipped over by the bikini depilation she had done before she left

with everything beautiful. So beautiful that last time, Lord, my whole life so very beautiful until that night I took my kids with me through the carwash. When we were already back home in the middle of a February thaw and rapid refreeze which had left the car a mud speckled mess. The night I said, hoping they would enjoy the treat:

— Listen guys, this is just like the tropical storms your Dad goes through in rainy season.

(1,3,2,4)

While I listened to them bouncing up and down on the back seat. As whoosh the water came on and doused the car all foamy and the windshield was hit by a bright orange brush, a blue, a yellow, a lime, all tropical colours, the grey of the water blocking vision the orange blue yellow lime

now the barely perceived movement of a guacamaya in flight now a soaked woman in her bright overblouse withdrawing into the door of a hut or jumping off the road as the convoy approaches. And then that womblike sense of enclosure that some of us hate and others adore when you're lucky enough to be in an enclosed vehicle with the water coursing over every inch, as blinding as any Canadian snowstorm only the worst passes quickly and hypothermia is no danger

except in the mountains; which means you just crawl along with hopes no idiot is coming fast behind you or you pull over and someone always has a pocket flask especially in a tight spot like that where there's nothing to be done about it, a clear trajectory

like the plane so that I always say why not, even if that same American did say putting her hand on my arm look friend you have to watch it because it always reminds me of nights by the fire and hot buttered rum

especially my own beautiful antique silver flask the wife got me for a birthday present before she decided I shouldn't drink, the one I have to declare at customs coming and going that I take anyway because I can always trace my fingers along its embossing and think of her, her elegant lines

the winking brilliance of the house as the water floods amorphous around us the lower branches slapping onto the windshield if it's really tight jungle where even a Land Rover maybe bogs down and we have to get out, our boots deep into the mud and pulling out with that sucking sound your prick makes accidentally in the middle of a really tight and active fuck and we hook the cable

around a tree to winch her through some of us staying in and some getting out, the last time I steered, flask in hand humming of course, an old drinking song a bit like the carwash singing along with the kids, a hundred bottles of beer on the wall ninety nine bottles of beer as I turn around to watch them bounce as we're pulled through on a track the grey steel moving with us, the reduced world of brush and sponge moving by, another trajectory

that starts to scare me because it won't change whether I steer or not, not in this controlled tropical detergent storm with the three of us snug and warm inside if only I'd closed the vents which turns it to oh shit and the kids laughing as I wish for a moment I could at least gun the car forward

or stop the winch or had some modicum of control remembered how to close them as the water rises soaking the old newspapers I left on the car floor. While the kids lift their feet in the back giggling even harder around their ice cream cones to say between gasps:

— Is this really what it's like Dad? And I almost shout back, of course all the time but I still can't find the little lever to close the vents.

(4,1,3,2)

And I know that it will take days for the rugs to dry out. And the papers I hadn't even clipped yet are ruined and besides the soapy shit has slopped into my shoes. So that I thank God now for the trajectory that determines we're about to be hit (whump) in the windshield by the waxing brush

and then it will be over. Over and done. Which is terrific I think just terrific so terrific that I stop fussing and relax my shoulders to put a smile back on my face about to turn to the kids again to say something comforting only (eeeeerrrnnh) the buzzer that says fasten your seat belts fasten your seat belts your door is open you've left your keys in the ignition (eeeeeeerrrrrnnnh) goes off and won't stop and I start

almost a jump I can feel it in the back of my neck. And I have to remind myself it's not the whistle of a rocket or a flare that there won't be soldiers waiting for us when the water stops to check the vehicle over

and our papers too; it can buzz all it wants and there still won't be any megaphone to tell us to stop or any rule that says I can't turn off the internal light I've turned on to look for the lever because at night all cars must give them a clear look inside to see what kind of subversives

or just how many they might be carrying, no one to shoot at you if you forget, this is just one small reminder of that feeling that can't be quelled that I am quelling now in the pit of the stomach that makes the joints buzz

louder than the buzzer that says no matter how in order your papers are no matter how much better it is to be in a car full of Americans this time Americans not just Europeans or Latins or fellow Canadians who don't quite weigh as much in the eyes of soldiers who've been brought up on saluting the Embassy, always that, the Embassy there is only one

Embassy, the American Embassy and none other than the American Ambassador which still doesn't eliminate the remote possibility that this bunch of boys in green is just a little bit crazy or knows somehow that this time you are going to interview a guerrilla commander, any guerrilla commander, there are always more than one of those, or that someone in your car will just snap

and yell at them and soldiers don't like being yelled at so God knows what they'll do; maybe that gives them definite evidence that you're in league with the communists only commies answer back, you never know what's in their heads maybe it's just a bad night and the woman next to you is attractive and they wouldn't want to leave any evidence and besides she's taking penicillin

for a terrible sinusitis she's developed with this unending rain and for all you told her not to bring any medicine because of that stupid student who thought that the fact that the bus routes across Central America still operated meant there were no problems crossing, there are hundreds of them like that looking for the imaginary country of Nam, with most getting through and living to tell their tales of the most dramatic form of tourism short of loading your wheel hubs up with dope and trying to cross Asia, only this one

when they took everyone off the bus and kind of shoved him up against its wall the way they always do, he had objected. He was an American citizen or some such and call his Ambassador. Only it was too far from town and why bother

he was carrying medicine. Mostly aspirin and Pepto-Bismal, but some anti-biotic or other too. For the guerrillas they said to each other of course which meant he just never got back on the bus. So that even if she does say:

— Hell, Wes, I'm press corps, still you never know. Especially with those legs.

(4,2,1,3)

And then there's having to drive all the way home with that buzzer going off in my ear and nothing to do for my nerves with the kids still laughing. So hard in fact that one of them hits me

in the back of the neck with her ice cream cone adding a cold shiver and a small slide into the kerb and the beginning of a skid to all that noise. Which makes me feel lucky just to be able to keep on driving long enough to get back to the house where I pull the fuse out after the buzzer won't stop even when I turn off the ignition and the kids are already on the merry-go-round animals under the bougainvillaea by the time I get inside

having a fight; over whether to play reporters in Central America or Tarzan and Sheena king and queen of the jungle with no me Jane for my young lady just round and round again making up for the immobility of the merry-go-round animals with yes no no yes off on on off until I've had enough of things you can't turn off and I just throw my wet shoes and socks and ice cream soaked shirt down the basement stairs toward the laundry and yell

for my wife to run a bath: the whirlpool please and lean against the wall and look down at my feet all blue dyed from my socks before I pad on up and get in through the foam and try to wash them carefully humming some tropical tune while I stick them up in the air like flags or the foam-flecked rocks at the edge of the Caribbean growing blue algae scrubbing them back to the colour of sand while I wait for my wife to bring me a drink, a double rye this time on the rocks, the same delicious hot to cold of sun in the tropics, no more rain or snow or stupid detergent suds in these sweet bubbles as the wash cloth goes in between the toes and out again searching out the shallow crevices

of the self with a gentle massage where blue dye still grows and something else too; whose bloom makes my stomach grow cold as the ice in the drink, while the cold spreads to my hands and the washcloth stops and grows cold in the air because it was so easy to forget

what the doctor had once told me between his don't worry and his it's perfectly harmless repeating that article almost word for word to inform me that the ones you do have to worry about are usually bi-coloured or faded and uneven, most often hidden from view like so many truly dangerous things, the secret jails of Guatemala I added smiling, in places where the big daddy sun who's supposed to act as triggering agent in skin cancer would never think of shining any more than this smaller daddy can think of scrubbing

retreating instead before the evidence my feet now a sudden treasure of possible though terrifying knowledge that I treat with utmost care drying them quickly but carefully patting them with the towel

the way I should have done the soaked papers I carried in from the car patting judiciously and never rubbing inside and outside and then a prayer that the pages not stick together, crossed fingers for being able to read those words to decipher those signs that seemed important whether or not I ever got around to them, even if I left them at the top of the basement stairs where I put them right before I took off my coat to hide them behind the closed door the way I do my feet

in warm down bootees because I need to know that the knowledge, all the references, are at my fingertips in case I ever need them to figure something out to jog my memory with some essential fact that I am always sure is there, something behind the data that won't go away, like I am suddenly sure nothing will go away, whether I try to decipher anything or not, no fact no event hidden in the symbols in those papers no possibility no inevitability hidden in the signs on my body will

go away until I almost scream with an expanding anxiety that says that these things will remain active to trigger some unexplained catastrophe make some story that will succeed in bringing down a way of life but whose background no one will ever report because its causes will remain hidden from us though bound to rebound into us to change or mutate something while we cross our fingers and tell ourselves over and over

that none of it will ever be more than superficial just ink on a page just marks on a body a harmless way to pass the time like my wife counting each spot while I read each word over and over until it tickled too much and I grabbed her and forgot about all those little letters in the paper those signs on me those pieces of information those syntheses and summaries and latest items

I was reading; like making myself a triple right after the double and another couple too before I go see the doctor to further protect my down and wool wrapped body against winter and knowledge so that it isn't panic that tingles in my arm this time as I ride

up the first three floors through the shopping mall on the escalator looking down at the scattered arms and legs sticking out among the reflecting glass, blues and reds and yellows and secret metal grey winks moving from place to place a procession a parade around and around and around the muzak buzzing out its dull rock as obedient shoppers go up one escalator and by the boutiques then down the other by more boutiques and up again yet another time to the other side now, what pretty things pointing across

the gap to where the colours seem brighter; then down again to the rhythm of the same little flashes barely visible from boutique doors as they open and close like the wide flash of hookers' smiles

on dark streets as the glass windows reflect back so that you can't see what called those shoppers inside so that you go closer to find when you get there a shop the same as the one you just passed on the other side which means that maybe you go in and maybe you move on and maybe you say good morning Madam

or afternoon Miss and I buy myself a new wallet for the wallet photos that I show to the salesgirl what a beautiful wife and such lovely children she smiles as the counter gleams and I think for a moment I should be buying the small Plexiglas stand up frame to sit by my bed in the hospital; because I can see it clearly pink or grey or green or blue pastel with its metal night stand in matching subtle tone that's never white because hospital white is out now especially for terminal patients who know they will never leave and my hand reaches out only to stop

in time to say a simple how pretty as she smiles brighter and tells me it would look lovely on a little night table a little pink or grey night table and I see it gleaming maybe a green night table and the clear Plexiglas winks like the smoke grey Plexiglas of the pay phones the mirror sides of the escalators and I see

how restricted my movement will be in that room: small circles one two three four accomplished by shifting my head from angle to angle three two one four. So that the faces of my family my own face reflected

two three four one would appear and reappear like the faces of the people in the park gathered around the ferris wheel looking up and waiting four two three one on the merry-go-round until one is missing. I am missing. And I say:

— Thank you Madam.

(3,4,2,1)

Only maybe I said *gracias* the way I did to that man who helped me down when the ferris wheel stopped. Certainly she looked at me strangely enough though maybe she knew I had been drinking. Or perhaps it was just the tears in my eyes as I put the pictures back before I went back out and followed them all up up and around and down; and wasn't the only one, not by far. There were bunches of them, those same people appearing again and again

at different points on the graph, up and down and around and around like the one in the classic lady's suit and tightly set hair each one in place silver-tipped chestnut like the manes on my carved lions just curled forward around the tight lips, another punk colours and spikes a black fake leather mini and purposely torn stockings white legs showing through

so much the pony with its polka dots and its stiff mane carved out as if flying and its bright coloured harness, the man too in the tiger striped shirt yellow and black and fierce bright smile grinning and turning to the rhythm of his own world what must be happening in his walkman while the other behind him

placid chews his cud almost lowing in his brown tweed three piece suit the one gleam of gold not his nose but his ear as his foot paws the stair: each one at her or his exact place one behind another up down and around the little octagonal garden of ficus trees shining in the artificial light; dark absorbing blue green behind bright repellent yellow green far below while others on benches lick phosphorescent ice cream in gleaming glass bowls and dull brown sugar cones, drink cappuccino in little porcelain cups seated on wrought iron chairs laughing until the music stops and I get off and continue upward on the stairs to avoid

any sudden stops; all those ups and downs of the stomach dodged except the last one caused by the quizzical look on the receptionist's face for how out of breath I was which makes her tell me how late it is, you're late Mr. Smithson as I sit down with the tingling still in my joints and no edge to look over or pattern to follow except a basic discouragement or disillusion sitting there with my arms down between my legs too tired to even open a magazine to take up

even one more image or story: how to cope with, the truth behind, not wanting any string at all to lead me out of the maze because now mine was one ending I no longer wished to have to predict not without 'and now Wes Smithson the author of' printed on the story that would bring down a whole way of life because there was so much anyone who had worked where I have worked should already have known or heard

the helicopters (whup whup whup whup) revving up behind in an offstage chorus that goes around and around the already well understood fact that you never believe anyone in authority who smiles to tell you it's nothing with those small short sounds

sharp out of mouths repeating and repeating no longer words but explosions in the mind (harm less go a way un un un com com com fort fort fort fort able faaaade) each one another blow the determined crack of the sniper's bullet or the rushed together breeze of machine-gun fire until you can't even hear go away any more but just hear blow away blow

away for the style in which more than one boy soldier has gone away stepping on a home-made mine somewhere out in the country where the population has already decided on the subversion of self-defense and so shortly

after telling that terrible story the one he knew he was never supposed to tell and telling it anyway not to you really but to the surrounding air as if he were just leaving it around somewhere for someone to pick up his voice somewhere between laughing and crying his balled fist pounding on your knee or was it your friend's? as he told how he had told the other soldiers in that village that he wouldn't shoot children that one thing I won't do I won't shoot children

he had said while his being barely more than a child himself only made his officer who had come up behind turn him around so that he could laugh right in his face while he took the safety off his uzi and aimed it right at that boy's head to make him an example to the rest the officer

repeating I will, I will; and laughing even more when later the boy obeyed his orders and did what he was told, exactly what he was told shooting anything that moved or knew how to which didn't even save the boy because he went away so soon after boom

as we walked behind such a special privilege to be there and him telling his story with his too adult laugh in his child's face, the beginning for a story to bring down a whole society a way of life become just another legacy for the bush together with his segmented body the fragments of self

going away. Up up up and away, away away over the edge of low brush up up and down again to where only the Devil with his special smile could pull back the bar, thank you for coming like the doctor looking and then grinning down between my toes on the inside edges

of my scrotum as his hand and eye pull each part into separate into segmented existence. Tiny little split off pieces of me at which he whistles and laughs. And mumbles:

— You certainly did pick up a case, Wes. Could they be ticks maybe? Tiny, underdeveloped perhaps? They're just like the ones I always got at home as a boy. Only so much smaller.

(1,3,4,2)

Only this time when he assures me that they're perfectly harmless even if he's never seen their like before I just want to say the way I have to my son since his second teeth came in, and maybe I shouldn't, teeth aren't after all Pinocchio's nose and even if rodent teeth never stop growing rabbits aren't quite the same but anyway I always do say it and want to say it to the doctor now: what big teeth you have Peter Rabbit. And I don't just feel him

lying to me, nibbling the garden of my self away with his words but eating up the world too. Aiding in its digestion with his teeth's solid raw bones set in blood red gums like the boy's femur where it had been separated from his hip. And I want to go on to mention to the good Doc that the ticks in underdeveloped countries are huge and fat

like the smiles of generals. Which is true enough except that there are too many kinds, a plethora just like the uniforms and the officers: big and small fat and thin dull and bright but always full up with the blood of others, of the people their slogans would say down there; yes a plethora I think

he will like that word, a wordsmith's word and then some jokes about them too: how they suck your blood like Mexican bureaucrats, the underling and the minister, a perfect Mexican arthropod in fact *la garrapata* I remember them so well from the first case I ever picked up in cattle country somewhere close to the Yucatan and Cozumel, lowland bordering jungle hot as hell and the first time I had been there with everything sweaty and itching, the big ones easy enough to find and not altogether unexpected, you looked as you scratched examining yourself in the last light of day but God, the terror of the little ones, minuscule really that wouldn't be told apart from freckles except when the critters packed up their little probosces and decided to move on and you could catch them in the act

small they were, tiny and medium brown and ravenous so that I didn't say anything to the Doc about being full of it because I wanted him to be right even if I knew better even if I was sure that these particular spots had migrated only in some other secret clandestine manner like guerrillas through the jungle

of my cells through the city streets of my capillaries so that I know but I don't say, mum's the word, shsh and let's go and a casual face on it for when you're walking with a contact and you don't want anyone to see that you share the secret of disbelief because after all it's so much safer

to believe them and pretend nothing ever happens there is no war the beaches are beautiful even with sand fleas or the jungle with wood ticks no one ever disappears and maybe these do itch and itch in the same way those others had done only stopping briefly when he rubs one

under his finger until it hurts and bursts and there's a stink and he laughs and it's easier to believe whatever anyone tells you than to think of the signs, of the meaning of the graffiti on the sides of buildings penetrated by bullet holes or the warning moles that itch moles that hurt moles that bleed, no longer small numb cherry red spots filled with blood but truly bleeding real red blood dripping between my toes the old newsprint spots bleeding from their black centres true bleeding hearts of darkness that made me smile and laugh

in turn and tight lipped move once more over to the window to try to control my scepticism to look down to get an overview, a long distance perspective that will calm my stomach and my mind until I can fool myself again make myself just go home and maybe have another or rip off a piece or at least do something that will conserve my peace of mind to help me shed my doubts once more into the tub again which would have been as easy as ever if I hadn't looked up from my favourite occupation of contemplating where precisely a bus moved not blue and silver this time but white

from the top white plastered on the sides, a nasty early spring morning all blowing white like the water against the car windows with everything that moved and much that didn't white on white on grey on white a tonal circling

circulating in the city around and around and that queasy feeling again, the grey roofs forcing my eyes away and up to look into the building opposite to comfort myself with bright plastic office furniture to meet instead, a trick of the aluminum thick air

my own reflection; a gleam of a face like the people on the escalator distorted and still and thick my own carved wood mask about to scream, what I still don't know, the mouth slightly open as I watch reflected from behind me his hand lifting like the hand on an escalator that waves at the friend below at another place on the circle a tentative gesture, hi or goodbye he must be smiling only I can't see his face it's dark or grey or turned away as he takes the scrapings from between my toes and places them on a slide and covers the slide and throws the dull aluminum instrument

into the gleaming aluminum autoclave, while I imagine he's whistling a whistle without a tune that places the slide with a bunch of others my moment of halting over as (whoosh) I feel myself falling back down

hard toward that ground, fragmented or segmented myself because I don't know if there will be anyone down there even the Devil to pull back the bar as I try to hold onto the plastic edge of the window the metal edge of the ferris wheel car so afraid to let go because who knows any more if the framework of the ferris wheel of the precise ordering of my house of my words of my suitcase of my costume of my life of everything I know can still hold

me in and take me back around again, up up and around again, one and three and two and four, three and four and two and one, or if this time I am bound for the ground. With no companion's hand on my arm to tell me it's all right it's all right it happens all the time, all the time

in these countries; and in those because I am left with just this tingling in my joints that is no longer the drink but signals that I know it only has to happen once for each of us. Nor is it the alcohol that slurs my voice as I speak

to the doctor but the knowledge that it's not a parasitology lab those slides are bound for. Because in the instant of my turning some few letters wrote themselves onto my mind and now read themselves back to me in an order that spells out biopsy

and melanoma on the label of his little box until I can see them clearly as the slur edges toward a scream. The mouth of the mask that is my face still reflected open in the glass where I wish I could leave it as I take my last leave of him.

— Well Doc, I say, still facing the snow covered grey on grey buildings, I hope this is it for a while.

(1,4,2,3)

And I edge out past the doctor to return to the mall to spend the afternoon with the lion and the tiger and the ox and the pony. To go around and around again as I smiled at them and waved and they waved back; up and down and around and wave and wave and wave

and wave. Only I couldn't get them to come to the bar with me no matter how I waved or gestured or to come closer to whisper their secrets no matter how I beckoned. Any more than I can get the secrets from those little creatures between my toes that big story that will tear a whole way of life apart out of the army or the edgy shantytown dwellers whose eyes look down and away and who never see a thing no matter how bright the moon or how often

I rephrase it; or the translator does with a slightly different form or intonation a mention of someone else we know who trusts us, we still can't change the run around and around again with their no, no, nothing

yes, maybe, something, someone is missing but they know nothing none of them saw that anybody took them a limited vocabulary that reaches its final limit in a shrug broad as if stretching; their muscles pulling against their bones like cats or the way you move when you wake up from deep sleep into the moment of taking yourself into account

of knowing that you are still present a body language way of saying all right, hey, I'm all right, I'm unharmed, none of them ever trying to reassure anyone else but just smiling fed cat smiles at you and the translator for all they may have gone hungry for days because they know as well as the next person and you do too that they will only stay unharmed by repeating that

no no nothing song and dance again and again and again and again so that you smile too and let them give it one more go round: everything around here all right, that's right okay meester okay? all right all right? what I say over and over around and around trying

to convince myself it isn't me down there that's an unknown universe as I overcome my squeamishness to look closely at those things between my toes around the edges of my balls even taking a mirror, all right all right, to observe the crack in my ass, breathing more freely to find that he was right that they weren't just spots, which was fine except that it didn't make them so easily excised either, things you just scrape off

the surface skin from right there on the very top layer digging the proboscis out of some small capillary and squeezing their filled to bursting bodies until they explode eight legs in sixteen different directions because they look more like tiny snakes minute vipers in tail biting circles more nauseating than the grossest ticks even by the light of a kerosene lantern and as well encysted as completely entrenched as the trichina I once ate by equally soft light in some marvellously spiced pork at a village wedding

gelatinous things that another newsman pointed out to me as I've always wished since that he hadn't, asking me to look at the little eggs in the meat noticeable as hell once you started to look for them easily a full quarter of an inch across so that we had popped a couple out

with our pocket knives; what your mother always told you about with her don't eat pork if it's still pink of the days when you frightened yourself with diagrams in biology books but never really believed anything even in a tropical country could be like that, the two of us feeling like boy scouts

with our Swiss Army knives a perfect experiment for the science fair at school emptying out some 35mm. slides from their plastic case and plopping the little balls in, so jelly like and giggling in a way boys always call by another name, sniggering or chortling our heads together like we imagine girls' heads in the girls' washroom as we readied ourselves to take them to the local medicine man, we always call them that, even when they have their American or European or even Russian degrees in specialties like parasitology or otorhinolaryngology up on the walls, more qualified for sure than that guy I've been going to with his everything will be all right it's harmless except in the end who cares

about qualifications it's off to the medicine man we said, our heads still together to find out what we already knew as he went so far as to let us look in the microscope at the little snakes biting their tails all snuggled up cosy in their tiny one bedroom cysts and laughed at us, as he poked one with a dull aluminum instrument and we shivered as it fell apart

before our eyes and he told us how very well cooked they were and how very tender, just the kind the country people recommended the best meat of all the meat with the eggs in it even if it wasn't Canada 'Grade A' like my juicy smooth oiled skin with the eggs in it and from a prime bullshitter those offspring

of some strange new parasite; perhaps about to hatch some stranger new reality I didn't want to face hidden just under the surface of my so well baked skin to make my hand reach again and again

for the medical sample cream he held out to me because even if it would do no good or you didn't need it anyway still you take it, you always take your medicine because no matter what there's always that attempt to do the 100% safest thing, to get that special confidence you get from drinking bottled water lukewarm Coke or beer no matter how much sicker it makes you, dehydration and alcohol or the days of purple nausea that caused my vision to blur

to green that followed taking that parasite killer for over-cooked trichina the two of us in the lower rungs, it seemed so right, of the heavyweight category the way I feel right now looking at my body or avoiding looking at it, such a light heavyweight this one that will never get the story which will bring down a whole way of life the vision blurred again and a desire to vomit so that I can no longer

gain confidence from doing it; spreading the cream and repeating the safest thing the safest thing rubbing at those old newsprint coloured blotches and their black black centres that aren't snuggled up little snakes with their tails in their mouths any more or even happily encysted

little round worms. These eggs, these seeds, if that is what they ever were, these spots these pimples these larvae they stretch now into waking: frog eggs becoming tadpoles in their safe jelly molds

they stretch and wind. To become squiggles and curves and straight straight lines; the beginnings of spirals or half octagons, the few perfect circles like black ringworm or a mouth held open before speech: images that make me put my own shoulders my whole body into the circle as I rub. And to never let my wife do it

even when she asks. Telling her that I like my privacy in the bath the way I always have and then humming to myself sometimes to show her that's all it is, or to convince myself the doctor is still right when he says:

— You're just gonna have to be more careful in those tropical countries. Between the ticks and the skin fungi it must be just hell.

(3,1,4,2)

Because it certainly does become uncomfortable with my feet not even fitting in my shoes. And it burns too. Up around the edges of my balls and my armpits sometimes, worse than that last sunburn on Cozumel and all over too. So that even if it makes me think of the first flare of the beginning fire after the gasoline is tossed on, how they do that to a lot of people I no longer bother

to reprimand myself. But just squeeze a few tears out of my eyes whose salt irritates my already raw face as I think of them in the middle of the villages upon occasion and always still alive, remarking acidly to no one at all to prove I still can how I suppose the *auto da fe* is easier with gasoline because you don't have to set up a pyre

just a cordon of soldiers. Because this is all just too uncomfortable for me to spend much time any more weighing moral questions: whether sado-masochism is all right between consenting adults or only when represented by gently tied and obviously unhurt women or young men in not too hard core skin magazines while I try, correct or not to feel the edge

of that terrible pain; because even that familiar anxiety won't come any more to accompany those thoughts and if I cry harder for the dissident intellectuals than for the peasants it is just out of envy because no book I write will ever be worth burning its pages crisping up in terrible but awe-inspiring pyres in the streets much less myself; it would occur to no one to do to me what's been done to more than one poet or journalist with gasoline and a match and a few soldiers to kick him to kick her to try to exorcise to excise all those words, to knock their ideas out of their heads and prevent their entering one's own, trying to spill them out to crush them to finally burn them to stop the contagion, and him or her with them because idea and person and word

have become the same; and only a complete burning will do which there's absolutely no reason to do to me, nothing I could possibly do could be that thorough or deeply felt or have such consequences I will never have that story that brings down a way of life that brings about a conflagration, I will only need something pink handled and superficial like my sweet electric torture, that needle with its pink handle burning out words or hearts or ideas with maybe just a little flash waiting like an old oven lighting with a small explosion when you're just down to the end of the match: eyebrows and eyelashes gone

along with this year's crop of words, at worst a beach in the tropical sun with first and second degree burns a little ooze to the flesh for a couple of days and then a peeling and new ones growing in, a fresh epidermal layer with bleeding hearts or heartless to fit the occasion like that last terrible burn I got despite my wife's warnings her constant for Christ's sake Wes, use the ointment

with me so stupid after all these years that I kept telling her it was all right I'd already had a lot of exposure I was used to it, as if anyone ever gets used to the tropical sun when even the tropicals wear big white shirts and wide brimmed hats, except it did feel so very good just to relax and I hate that oily sandy feeling the cream leaves so who could bother and the fact is it kept on feeling good right up until that first drink after sunset when the dehydration hit me the burning up and dizziness and the sand rubbing in my shorts the way it is now a constant sensation

of sand in the shorts only this time it won't peel nor will I be able to let my wife peel me the way she used to love to do telling me you're a snake Wes, squirm and shed your skin like a snake Wes, an old snake Wes and the new skin so very pink beneath and so tender especially when she would pull too hard and the dead skin would rip into the still living and I would jump or squeal and she would kiss me to make up and I would fondle her under the negligee she still wears to attract me like tropical foliage

only I can't any more; when all I want to do is walk around the house naked waiting for the new skin to come in to stop me feeling so raw while I no more believe it will than I can believe I will ever be able to grow a new set of words of ideas of bleeding hearts to let me go out and get the story that will bring down a whole society a way of life, there's no room anywhere

among all those creatures that refuse to budge while they grow and prepare themselves for something beyond my ken no place for even the most innocuous words with which to form the fluffiest little story that couldn't possibly get any-one burned, something not even worth a bikini depilation or pulling off the dead skin or singeing the split ends

of the hair; though I still try at least a little really I do no matter what my wife says or my kids think wondering why it's been so long since I've left except to put on my old hiking shorts to hike into the garden or stand barefoot and thoughtful looking out into the distant closeness of the lilac hedge with its green protectiveness so like the passion flower but without that stiff that hieratic and stubborn sense of hierarchic almost military order, the lilac's small bunched flowers saluting

no one their still spring attempt at bloom a vitality that will remind me occasionally that there are still a few things more to do so that I mumble to myself gotta go now and deadline coming up and assignment to move on and important interview

down on the mall to help me walk out the garden gate to find myself soon after old fashioned sugar cone in hand trying once more to get their stories out of the pony and the tiger and the lion and the ox as I ride up and down and over and around and whisper my secrets across the infinite space between

the glowing aluminum and the mirrors to see if they will reciprocate in front of the admiring audience there below, the people so little and far away with their ice creams and their cappuccino as the ball of pink cold drops out of my reach as we pause at the top and I laugh as it falls

down and hits the ground and everyone looks up and there is just enough time to look over at pony and ox and lion and tiger, one moment for a word and a gesture across the gap as they signal back grim and secret

and silent fingers to lips up and down and around and around; and around and around until I understand that they are trying to say that an important breakthrough is coming up for all of us. So that when my agent calls with a new assignment I too put my finger to my lips

lowering my feet, from their position up or soaking as high spring approaches with the lovely hinted scent of the summer to follow and I get up to walk out all the way to the lilac hedges and stick my nose into the completely open blooms and wiggle my toes into the grass. And I hear my wife's voice drift out through the open glass patio doors:

— No, he's laid up he can't come to the phone. Something he picked up in the tropics.

(2,3,1,4)

While I drink whatever remains in my glass as I stand there in the shadow of the purple blossoms and the green leaves. Before I amble back to where the merry-go-round animals await their final assembly under a green and white canopy to match the patio umbrella, their final attachment to an inflexible steel frame all of them about to be linked together once more

the distances perfect. Without knowing why it's the one thing I feel up to since it seems pretty hard work even to put down the drink to wrestle with the kids the way I used to do whenever I first got back laughing hard with them like that first moment at the airport, the door opening on grins I was so afraid to never see again the way they whisper to each other as if I've just gotten back from somewhere

as I grab them: hey Daddy's back. And then they're so helpful wanting to get this thing turning around asking day after day when the motor is coming and I want to know too because it's such a good time touching and fondling those animals, the smooth time worn many coated wood, it's so good to know that soon I will be able to follow them around to ride them through space so that I won't have to escape

down to the mall any more for my rides with the ox and the lion and the pony and the tiger because the tiger is right there near the lilac and the ox over where I can see the bougainvillaea through the glass door when I sit on his back and fondle him in his precise position on the frame as the local craftsman fits together the tongue and groove wood floor and says great stuff you have here Mr. Smithson and whistles between his teeth and pats the pony on the rump all of them so lovely together and him in love

with solid wood and the workman's chaos around us, crates and tool boxes and small pieces of pointed metal or of wood nuts and bolts and pegs and screws and dowels and routers and saws and blades and pliers and ratchets and other dull aluminum instruments reminders of something and of nothing

of pain and history and maintenance and construction and change that make it a long time before anyone notices anything new or strange or changed on me standing there in the middle of it a tall glass in my hand humming a wordless witless tune around and around shirtless and barefoot or with an athlete's sleeveless shirt its bright number one or two or three or four printed on front and back to go with the many numbers lying around the ones that show how

to put things together: matching tiger to tiger and pony to pony and lion to frame so that nothing is noticed except when my wife comes out to inspect, none of this dirty work for her in her flowered sundress and huge floppy flower strewn straw hat to ask again and again

will it be ready soon? pondering when it will become the unique part of the decor that the craftsman and I have promised her the gift she finally accepted by chucking the ox under his beautiful round chin saying the envy of the neighbourhood yes, yes; with a faraway smile for me before turning again to look around her carefully as if counting each bolt, the ways in which each object has changed

position from the last time she carried drinks out on her Plexiglas tray looking back at me as if I were part of them, as if she were finally starting to accept me just being there, and sitting on the animals and disappearing for hours at a time to make my rendezvous to ride up and down and around with the lion and the tiger and the ox and the pony chucking me under the chin too and kissing me

on the cheek or neck looking down at my feet and saying yes, better better, he'll soon be better this will soon be all cleared up or maybe it's cleaned up

to the craftsman or even to a wider audience just never to me only patting me on the arm and going away, better better it will soon go away and looking at the sky her own words up and down and around and over me as she examines it all picking up each piece looking at each number to find its match

and putting it down, soon be finished soon be better we'll be able to clean up the mess as I looked off into the distance trying to focus the faint purple of the lilac blooms match them to the colour of the thick twilight sky as if they too had a number as if it were all just a puzzle and all I had to do was match everything one to one or tiger to tiger or lion to lion or bloom

to sky and me to better. So that it still didn't occur to me to think that I was the puzzle. Or the breakthrough. That I was what would soon be finished. Just as soon as all the parts were assembled all the information matched to its correlative. Not until the day that as my wife held my hand one of the children said from his position lying on the ground observing the lion's mane and the sky behind:

— Hey, Sis, look. Now Daddy has a funny freckle like a baby snake on his heel.

(4,2,3,1)

Which makes it definite at last that I've been believing it too long, far too long for all that I've laughed and made cynical asides. Maybe since I started this job maybe since school. From the first 'A' I ever got on a composition or maybe from even before

the first four letter word I ever spoke, with the first symbol I ever deciphered. But it's enough of this, just enough this always looking for the right prescription. Whether from a doctor down there extending me that remedy for trichina or giving me his wide smile and thees ees eggzacly thee theen for guat joo got Mr. Smeeethsawn while handing me a medical sample of some anti-biotic for bronchitis pneumonia meningitis influenza salmonella diarrhea gonorrhoea septicemia dysentery typhoid outlawed ten years ago in the States and God knows when back home or it's the IMF prescribing belt tightening to people so skinny their belts already look like my wedding ring with someone always saying it will all be better

tomorrow, just one of these and it will be better tomorrow pain and poverty better tomorrow except of course it never is they just perfect new ways of hiding it, shantytowns behind bright painted walls old people in homes terminal patients in beautiful clinics only enough is enough of this hiding myself from myself to know without my wife having to say it again, repeating Wes Wes, this can't go on Wes, that I must go for a second opinion, find some other escalator or elevator or a long wide staircase to follow up and around until I enter another office to look down on the minute people, unable to distinguish there below pony or ox or lion or tiger which doesn't mean I really expected to finally get on this merry-go-round that takes me around and around and up and down the green the purple garden or even my ground floor room with its green walls and its purple lamp shade its pale blue sheets where they still come

each day and say yes yes, we'll know soon, very soon, soonsoon soonsoon, we'll have the answer soonsoon as they clap me on the shoulder and they look away or they write something down and they say just a few more days and don't worry and it's all right it's just for observation as they look away and they walk through the door and they tell the nurse to come for me to help me walk or to wheel me away as I try not to remember those men

who walked the long deep rugged corridors of those posh hotels where international human rights conferences were hosted short turning themselves halfway down as if by instinct no break in their conversation never going out of only recently imaginary bounds after so many years of soonsoon we'll know soonsoon what you did soonsoon I'm sure it's all a mistake a man of your standing in the community after all but orders are orders you know we have our orders the way the nurse says

doctor's orders, you know Mr. Smithson, you must stay on the path you must stay in the wheelchair if you want to go out in the garden we'll have to strap you in I'm very sorry but you do remember the last time when you fell over getting up to smell the flowers and how long did you lie there and we don't know do we? I'm very sorry Mr. Smithson poor Mr.

Smithson but we're sure it will be over soon very soon and this time

so am I; which I try to tell them but they don't understand they just ask for stories for all those interesting anecdotes I must have stored up in my brain saying why don't you tell us a story isn't it time

for today's story? until even my wife joins the chorus that tries to egg me on to push me over into familiar words into the same safe vocabulary that will help me regrow an unmarred epidermal layer as she tells me she has just watched Harvey on Channel 4 and that woman Rosalyn Whatsername I'd told her so much about, such terrific photos for a rather mediocre article of Joe's in the *New York Times Sunday Magazine* which was nothing

so good as mine she says winking, absolutely nothing so good as yours would have been on the same topic even if they wouldn't take it. Because that was after all my job to do. The definitive article with all the info, the lowdown, I think she uses. And such good photographs from such a good photographer. Only it's too late now.

— But one day soon she says, you'll get it together. You'll turn it all upside down on them. I just can't wait till you're writing again.

(4,3,1,2)

Real stories I know she wants to say. Not this garbage these incomprehensible symbols on my pad; this stuff no one could possibly understand. So that I am sure she is asking herself why it had to be this, couldn't it have been something else instead of this? as she takes the paper from the afghan on my lap. Removing it easily from my feeble trembling hands that can't even push the wheelchair any more so fast across the lawn the wheels going around and around and up and down and over and around and back to my room until I don't know

which it is my merry-go-round circle of ox and tiger and lion and pony or my own little ferris wheel with each metal rim up up and over with one slightly flat on one side so that I feel each turn up up over and whup. Whup and whup and whup and whup, one and two and three and four and always the sense of my stomach

falling away; away away away like when I remember what my wife has said and I look at the drawings on that page, at those dreadful tangled squiggles that I make that try to comprehend

something I can no longer explain, so that I become so agitated when no one understands that I lift my arms up and down and up and down, up and over and even around while my wife says there there I didn't want to upset you; and she pats my cheek and bites her thumb because she feels so guilty for what she has said about my efforts; which doesn't make her understand or even try because she doesn't know she can't know anything about it which means she even kisses me on the cheek before she grabs up her purse to leave and she talks in front of me as if I'm not there as if I'm the one who doesn't understand when she doesn't

understand a word the interns say to her about the disease the course of the disease, its supposed aetiology or prognosis, about how certain cancers home to certain specific parts of the self, telling her there are certain little encoded sugars like little tags or ingrained commands orders always obeyed that guarantee they will go one place

and not the other, even draw her little diagrams that make her nod and smile, reassured, yes, yes, it looks so nice yes, that must be it, nicer than my squiggles by far for all the doctors' words the residents' diagrams the interns' drawings mean no more to her as they explain that there must be some kind of basic code for those terrible old newsprint coloured spots with their black centres that they just haven't broken yet, not yet

but soonsoon and I can't understand what they're waiting for it's really so simple so obvious now that it makes me want so bad to tell them that I twist up my face into a ferocious or a tired or a placid or a superior mask like tiger or pony or ox or lion because I have known ever since the resident took up the magazine my wife had left on the little table that comes up over my bed, the magazine that has dropped out of my hands

so many times as I tried to lift it, to look at my merry-go-round on the cover, the grinning face of the lion right there in the foreground, "A Very Special International Garden" or something it's called if I remember right from what my wife read to me talking as if to herself about how the house had been featured in *Canadian Homes* with the merry-go-round the *piece de resistance* of course, the photo where her own face grins from over the ox's back her delicately manicured hand

on its rump to begin on page 24 her final triumphant pony mounted entrance onto her world of the page taking up her rightful place riding around and around and around and up and over and down with the lion and the tiger and the pony and the ox following or leading or under her in black and white

and colour all of them smiling as they leave sculpture in the round and the go round of time to attain the plane, walking or riding from four dimensions into a closed world of two as the doctor takes the magazine without even looking

at me, and rolls it up and slaps his other hand with it while his eyes wander back to my body, measuring and weighing as if I had no dimension at all were so much dead meat with me unable to tell him that I have discovered what he has failed to that I am the one who has the info the lowdown the lead

for the big story that will tell it all that will bring it down that will change forever a way of life while I have to listen to him turn to the intern whose head has just appeared in the door to say something about how, you know, this guy had it all and then to watch him carry it off tucked there under his arm, a picture piece on all I had without understanding anything about it or why it has happened to me although he does manage to give me the last piece of the puzzle the last cipher in the code by starting to talk about women by saying how my wife is a looker, a beautiful piece

of that all that I had, or maybe it's only I'd like to fuck'er or another one on those pages it's always hard to tell now but the next thing I know he and the intern are rubbing their index fingers along something on that smooth surface and the subject at hand is the perfect fuck

how it just gets you all over: it's a mind fuck as well as a skin fuck, a mucous membrane fuck and an endocrine gland fuck and a digestive organ fuck, a competitive medical vocabulary build-up word after word with each one more rapidly thrown out because they both have to show they know their stuff as the index fingers move up and back faster and faster until the intern says that it's like the embryo back at the very beginning when brain and skin skin and brain and all the nervous tissue were all the same organ

feeling and thought and perception the same organ. Which makes them take their hands from the page and slap each other on the back or was it the hands? and disappear not quite into the sunset but out of my little green cell into the yellow orange hall taking away wife and children and lion and tiger and ox and pony; until I don't mind

any more the gentle pitying smiles they give my wife as they tell her they don't know that they have no real idea but they're working on it they're not ruling anything out given where I've been but cheer up there's still hope because I know now that they will never know because they just don't have that reporter's sense

of where the real story is that will bring it all down of how to get the lowdown on what will blow it wide open that no one's nose will ever be better than mine for sniffing out the real dirt that will change it all because they've given me the one missing piece the way sources so often do

without even knowing it: the burning knowledge of what had been so very subtly wrong all along is now mine because once more, so typical of the human being, we had overlooked the obvious. Which means that I will recover for just one minute

my sense of humour. My sense of the juxtaposition of the rare and the common that brings out just the right cliche for the most peculiar moment, that sense that got me through so many years in this business in Central America and elsewhere. So that it will be me not them who sits up as far as he can in the bed to shout:

— Eureka, Eureka, I've found it.

(4,3,2,1)

To find that only another messy disarticulate sound modulates from my throat. A sound that chokes me on my own saliva and that makes me laugh. Until tears come to my eyes and my body shakes the bed and some liquid emerges warm from somewhere there below because it is

really so funny. If you have any sense of the ironic, any sense of the displaced, the disoriented the just slightly askew. Because how can I explain to them without words about those words. That it's words again that have made fools of us all. Because that's what those spots are you know: little letters. Thick and thin, gothic and italic and helvetica and bold. Letters letters letters letters a secret special alphabet full of special secret letters becoming words and phrases

and encoded sentences. That get longer and longer and longer and dig in and take over and wrap around my scrotum and my toes and my nipples and my neck and my ears, moving on and homing in and journeying far and metastasizing their way to my brain because it was once the same organ and nothing

can ever be only skin deep. No matter what anyone says, which is why they invade now. All those unwritten stories those undigested incidents those unfelt words at first indecipherable and unpunctuated and now perfectly clear absolutely clear paragraphs that I can see in the mirror at the base of my spine when the nurse turns me over to have my bath; hard things that occupy my brain already too big and too powerful to be redigested or denied to be put back into the easier words that I always thought were all that mattered of language, to be shoved back onto the epidermal layer or made to occupy their proper metaphysical state

between the synapses, instead of becoming concrete heavy letters carved deep in the cerebral cortex from a reality I have never fully understood to make it impossible for anyone to ever find a way to expel those creatures from the centre of my being, no way to help me invent a different skin because it's already a new vocabulary beyond my ability to decipher its explosion in my brain to feel or understand its process, disassemble the pieces deconstruct the phrases dissolve the tumour cells

back to their components, to make my own matter mine again my own cells to listen once more to my own body's commands or even any way at all to get a take on it a way to make it read with all the questions I am left with for a writer so much more introspective than myself and me the only one left

in my world to ask them of, so that inadequate as I am before this challenge still I must do something to avoid the blank void of that passion flower purple powdery painted wall that attempts to absorb me into nothing not a mark on it not even a small crack on which to hang some fantasy if not the story that will bring down a way of life so that I who avoided introspection so long wind down into that circular attempt around and around and up and down to try to find

meaning; or at least have a reason to be here to chase the solution to my puzzle the continuation to my story. Only to find that whatever I seek digs deeper and deeper into the patternless layers of that growth on epidermis and peritoneum in cerebrum and medulla to take refuge in a place where I know there is no help in knowing

that language, though it may be of sorts a virus, a small threaded DNA of its own, a substance never truly mine, is not of itself a cancer. Where there is no use at all in repeating:

— But it can't be a cancer.

(4,3,2)

Because I do know, because for the first time in my life I have looked closely. I have spent the last few weeks looking closely and I know now exactly how much language is capable of and that, like all of us it is not always what it should be. Something that grows and changes responding to its own rules with a profound internal complexity and an external shell as tough and resilient as the letters of the alphabet. That becomes slowly other through successive layers

of self whether ever quite as complicated as a well ordered and orchestrated parasitic or bacterial growth each self-contained unit with its organelles both me and not me at once or always more straightforward and streamlined and beautifully baroque to the electron microscope like one of those viruses with a letter name: T or L or O or P. Because whether you choose to recognize it or not it turns

on us sometimes. Like a herpes attack perhaps: facial not genital the simplex or complex of the solar plexus always so much more obvious, but in both cases creatures living somewhere in the ganglia, safe and happy lives perhaps you could call them normal anyway

in their little nerve cell houses so far from the skin, from the scene of the action it would be safe to say until suddenly a momentary stress calls them to change location to look conditions over in the instant before the wheel starts moving again maybe or the plane stabilizes or the soldier lowers his gun, when they go into action in a fast viral migration out to the skin to the very last flaking edge of the epidermal layer the corner or fleshy bottom of a suddenly dry lip

with just a tiny itch as you find yourself speaking words that never belonged to you, words you did not know or did not know you knew, their little sounds their little letters all in an order that would never have occurred to you, not to put together in quite that way never mixed with so much feeling that help

should come before me and after God and then there's the part about home, let me go home, and me saying it, an irreligious man repeating just this once God and then I'll give you anything, me who never did take any of His Commandments seriously or even His asides like that whatsoever be done to the least of these, that it could be contagious, all those things that happened to them, whatever them it was, just thinking that it was done and that was that and nothing ever to do

with those that were neither last nor least and anyway on the periphery because I always did think I was apart from all those realities, I flew so high above them, I took pills to immunize me from them drinks to build up antibodies cynical phrases to maintain quarantine beaches and swimming pools

to wash them off so that I felt protected no matter how much I wanted to taste them now, now, a little lick and a special flavour deep in the throat, still I knew it couldn't affect me because after all I never did know before that brain and skin were once the same organ that there was this interconnection between inside and outside that maybe would have stopped me from doing what I have done that would have kept me riding

around and around and up and down, on lion and tiger and pony and ox eating good down home gourmet ice cream whose flavour was obvious right there on the package and not listening to helicopters or fans (whup whup whup whup) or at least paying them no attention: doing anything to avoid

such a lesion; what was perhaps such a tiny first lesion in that moment that those words mumbled out of my mouth and my knuckles went white and my companion's hand came to rest on my arm and I hardly noticed it occurring because who would ever guess that it could lead

to this: a state in which all is lesion and nothing I can say is recognized any more, not by me not by anyone as it comes out of those terrible massed words that were never mine that I never knew to say that have metastasized to my brain to all my ganglia until I am helpless

here howevermuch I wave my arms around and around and up and down because no one understands and I think it is dreadfully unfair of God really it is especially since I never meant to call on Him so how can He do this now calling in my debt when I am almost home because even if I did say I would take anything He wanted to dish out if He just gave me that period of Grace to get the story that would blow it wide open still

those weren't my words; none of those words I wrote were ever truly my words, they were someone else's all of them and those last just the first sign of this disease in which brain and skin become once more the same organ in which inside and outside perception and thought are one and nothing can be separated or said because He never did do it before, give me that Grace to find the story that would bring down a whole society a way of life He just kept playing tricks, played another joke it must be very funny to be God, His final joke on me this calling in my debt in these little not even monthly but daily hourly instalments of tiny letters in helvetica and selvatica and eloquentia and bold while He gives me this story

that would blow everything wide open, an entire world now when I cannot explain its implications in a way that would help to discover a vaccine that would hinder the development of this syndrome an anti-biotic to reverse it even a small bleeding heart to build up antibodies to stabilize such a terrible condition because there is no turn of phrase to construct a final immune barrier now when I will never be able to redigest this experience to put it into words that might help me to express ever again no matter how clear the day the difference

between dateline storyline byline wordcount and the blue blue pink blue purple blue green blue clear blue tenuous blue dense blue sky; with the trees rustling and the birdwings whupping and the lion and the ox and the tiger and the pony moving

stiff-jointed still-faced around and around and up and down there below as the ferris wheel starts over and I let go of my companion's arm and I smile and I smile my eyes wide open the wind pressing my face because even if I want to yell out how good it is to be here to be present in the world without words or excuses or fantasies or stories still there is no way to formulate

even that with my tongue unable to find its place so that I cannot even take on something as brief and melodramatic as Terry Fox's run any last terrible long distance exertion for those who might yet develop this syndrome because in the end we are all exposed none of us are immune from savouring the reality of others and never taking responsibility for it making it ours inside and out until we can never know which vicarious thrill or hurt contains the trigger mechanism and I have no way to wake into roar or hiss or moo or whinny the lion and the tiger and the ox and the pony

stuck on their metal frame with its custom made motor the people on the escalator going up and down and round and round always in the same place the same position the same pose in the same photograph with the same caption at the same intervals with the same angular momentum, nothing that could save any of them not my wife not my kids not the man in the tiger striped shirt stuck in magazine or video game or walkman or idle conversation from these terrible lesions, from their subsequent or consequent development their explosive multiplication that leads inexorably

to this one same incoherent ending because even if I now know so much more than the rest even I do not know exactly what happens to start it whether it is brutality superficiality overexposure or the simple refusal to believe, thank You God for another trip home

that any of it matters; all I do know is that it is too late now that I ignored the symptoms far too long, that terrible queasiness as I sat in those rooms watching the fans go round and round one and two and three and four four and three and two and one thinking of helicopters and whores was allowed to go on until it is too late

for me, for even the smallest remission because as I sit here not in my hotel but my hospital bed listening to the room's three bladed fan that spins too fast for me to see I realize that after all the time

I put in all those years of work I did still I never paid close enough attention to piece together the story that will bring down a whole society a way of life because I do not even yet have the answer despite all my data from all my impeccable sources to that one key question I will now never be able to ask:

— What precisely is the carcinogen?

(4,3)

A search in which I know my wife would help if she could but all she sees when she walks in the door is arms waving up up and over and down and around legs going in smaller circles. So that she refuses to look at me and asks after the magazine as if expecting an answer will still at this stage automatically net her the right one, and then answers her own question while poking around under my pillow saying now if I were a big colourful garden magazine

where would I have gone. Never taking into account even the remotest possibility that my gestures, all those signs and symbols and signals even now might mean something might be trying to hint at something which maybe she could understand if she just didn't sit down

next to me distracted and humming the magazine now in hand the index finger pressing delicately on the pictures as she bites her lips and tears come to her eyes and she turns toward me on the bed and cuddles my large and ragged leonine head with its now slobbering mouth which she wipes with her own small hankie before she says there there soonsoon better soon pressing my mouth

between her breasts everything all right, you'll see, better better as she turns again and tosses her head, a delicate little thoroughbred whose mane surges forward over her face and back as she squares her shoulders like a little girl in a lace dress, she is wearing a Mexican lace dress, about to recite a poem in the class assembly. Who focuses her eyes over the heads of her audience just like the teacher said to do, you don't look at them if you don't want to get nervous, fixing her stare right in the purple blue wall behind my head gesturing with one hand as she announces:

— Don't worry dear. You will have your day. They say they're going to name the illness after you. Smithson Syndrome. Imagine that: Smithson Syndrome. The Channel Four factorum variant of Newsprint Melanoma.

(4)

Only I know now that it does not matter what the byline is or even what you say if the audience does not understand the story. Because it may well bring down a whole way of life blow an entire society wide open without their comprehension but they won't be able to make another whether or not my name comes out in all the papers, whether or not they broadcast it on all the airwaves unless we can still stop this thing

from blowing them up up and over. With their expressions forever fixed their mouths eternally open the multi-coloured layers of all they have known or experienced clinging unnoticed layer on layer to their skin as they go around and around and around and around, one two three four, up and down on the merry-go-round, the lion, the tiger, the ox, the pony. Down into speechlessness:

— Whup whup whup whup.